THE GLASS ARROW

West Dorling is a quiet, remote village. So what brings three men to live thereabouts at practically the same time? None of them seems to pursue any professional employment, yet they live in some style. When a local learns their secret and threatens blackmail, the three meet to discuss this threat. But on arrival, two of them find the other lying dead, shot through the heart by a glass arrow. Before long a second has died in the same manner. Who is the mysterious archer and why use *glass* arrows . . . ?

GERALD VERNER

THE GLASS ARROW

Complete and Unabridged

LINFORD
Leicester

First published in Great Britain

First Linford Edition
published 2014

A catalogue record for this book is available
from the British Library.

ISBN 978–1–4448–1835–2

Published by
F. A. Thorpe (Publishing)
Anstey, Leicestershire

Set by Words & Graphics Ltd.
Anstey, Leicestershire
Printed and bound in Great Britain by
T. J. International Ltd., Padstow, Cornwall

This book is printed on acid-free paper

1

Dr. Chambers' Premonition

The big, ruddy-faced man at the high desk laid down his pen and looked across the little charge room at the noisily ticking clock on the green-washed wall before him.

The room was small and low-ceilinged, for the police station at West Dorling had originally been a labourer's cottage, and the conversion to its present use had been carried out as economically as possible by a thrifty-minded council.

Sergeant Akeman was a very large man with short, clipped grey hair, and bushy eyebrows that jutted out over the steel rims of his spectacles.

The day was drawing to a close and he was not sorry. In another hour his relief would arrive and he would be able to go home to the supper of hot sausages and mashed potatoes that his buxom wife was at that moment preparing for him. It was his favourite meal — sausages and mash, with a pint of beer to wash them down.

He had picked up his pen to finish the laborious entry he was making in the Occurrence Book when the door opened and a man came in. His long raincoat was wet and shining and he took off his dripping hat and shook the water from its brim as he approached the desk.

'Good evenin', doctor,' greeted the sergeant heavily. 'Nasty night agin, ain't it?'

'Beastly!' grunted the newcomer. 'I suppose it'll stop raining one of these days.'

He pulled out a handkerchief and wiped his face and neck.

'I thought we was in for a dry spell this mornin', too,' remarked Akeman, shaking his head, 'but it didn't last. Ow's poor Joe Ollen, sir?'

'He's not in any danger, but he's unconscious, and will be in bed for some time,' answered Doctor Chambers. 'Compound fracture of the right knee-cap and head injuries. I hope you find the brute who did it!'

The sergeant pursed his lips.

'Nobody saw the car, so it ain't goin' to be easy,' he said dubiously. 'That was always a dangerous bit at the bottom of the 'igh Street there. You'd 'ave thought they'd 'ave stopped, though, wouldn't yer? They must 'ave known they'd 'it somethin'.'

'Some of these people aren't human!' growled the young doctor angrily. 'Ollen might have been killed for all the driver of that car knew — or cared. Still,' — his voice changed and he looked quizzically at the old sergeant — 'it helps you fellows to justify your existence. Barring street accidents you don't get much to do in a sleepy place like this, do you?'

'No, you're right there, sir,' agreed Akeman, with a slow smile. 'Nothin' much ever happens — though we did have a burglary once,' he added, his smile broadening into a grin.

'A real one?' asked Chambers derisively.

'Yes, sir. Up at Lord Hillingdon's

place,' replied the sergeant, 'though they didn't get away with nothin'. 'is Lordship surprised 'em, and shot the eye out of one of 'is ancestors!'

'That was before my time,' said Chambers. 'I don't remember anything as exciting as that happening while I've been here.'

'No, that was — let me see — eighteen months ago,' said the sergeant, gazing thoughtfully at the ceiling, 'and you've only been 'ere a matter of — 'ow long sir?'

'A year and three weeks,' put in the other.

'As long as that?' Akeman seemed surprised. 'Why, it only seems yesterday like that you took over old Doctor Bridgers' practice when he died.'

'It seems long enough to me,' said Chambers dryly. 'They're a hale and hearty people in West Dorling, Akeman, and time goes slowly when you haven't much to do.'

'I've often wondered, sir,' said the sergeant, 'why a young feller like you ever came to a place like this. I should 'ave

4

thought one of the big towns 'ud 'ave suited you better.'

''We can't all be choosers,' retorted Chambers shortly, and his good-looking face clouded.

'Myself,' went on the sergeant conversationally, 'I wouldn't change fer no man. But then I was born and bred in the district. They may get more excitement and such like in London and the bigger places, but I've got me bit of garden when I'm off duty an' I'm satisfied.'

'You may get some excitement round here before long,' said the doctor seriously. 'I've got an idea something 'ull blow up one of these days.'

'Meanin' between Mr. Baldock and Mr. Dinsley?' inquired the sergeant shrewdly.

Chambers nodded.

'Yes,' he replied. 'And old Flood.'

Akeman rasped his big chin with the tips of his thick fingers musingly.

'Queer 'ow them three seem to 'ate each other,' he said, after a pause. 'Don't seem no reason for it, neither, do there?'

'They hate each other because they fear

5

each other,' retorted the doctor. 'Have you ever seen them together?'

The sergeant shook his head slowly.

'No, I can't say as I 'ave, sir,' he replied, after giving the question his considered attention.

'Well, if you had,' said Chambers, 'you'd realize what I mean. Although they're always snarling and arguing, each watches the other like a cat eyeing a dog. And then there's Gormley, a smooth, slimy little rascal, who says nothing but just rubs his hands and watches. You mark my word, Sergeant, there'll be some trouble before long.'

'What sort of trouble, sir?' asked the interested Akeman, and Chambers shrugged his shoulders.

'I can't tell you that,' he replied. 'Perhaps they'll start killing each other. But there'll be trouble. You can sense it! I'm sorry for the girl, Dinsley's daughter. I believe she realizes that something 'ull happen before long, too.'

'Now it's funny you should say that, sir,' said the sergeant. 'My wife was only sayin' the same thing the other night. She saw Miss Ilene in the village and she said she looked as if she's got a pack o' trouble.'

The young doctor nodded.

'I thought she was looking pretty worried when I saw her last,' he said. 'Maybe that's because she's got Dinsley for a father.' He stopped suddenly and chuckled. 'Akeman, we're gossiping like a couple of old women! Most unprofessional conduct.' He gave his hat a final shake and put it on, pulling it down over his eyes.

'I don't see no 'arm in a bit o' gossip, sir,' said Akeman, his eyes twinkling behind his spectacles, 'so long as it don't 'urt no one.'

'Well, I don't think we've been malicious,' remarked Chambers. 'Except perhaps about Gormley. But then you can't think of him without.'

'I must be getting along,' he said, buttoning up his raincoat. 'Good night, Sergeant.'

'Good night, sir,' said Akeman cheerily.

Doctor Chambers came out of the small entrance to the station house into the pouring rain and hesitated for a minute, debating with himself whether he should take the short cut through Longman's Spinney or the longer way round by the High Street.

He lived in a small house facing the village green, and the footpath would save him a quarter of an hour, a consideration, for he was both tired and hungry. It would be a morass after the almost incessant rain of the past few days, but he decided he couldn't very well get either muddier or wetter than he was.

He set off along the gloomy road, splashing his way through the puddles that had collected in the hollows of the uneven surface, and presently came to the stile that marked the beginning of the footpath. It was very dark here and he took out the torch, which he always carried, and switched it on. The light was feeble, for the battery was at its last gasp and he had forgotten to renew it, but it was sufficient to show him the narrow track that twisted through the spinney. Halfway along he began to wish that he had decided on the longer route. The mud was inches deep and slippery, so that he had difficulty in keeping his balance, and in consequence his progress was slow. To add to his discomfort, when he had completed two-thirds of the journey, his torch gave out entirely, leaving him in pitch-black darkness.

A short distance ahead he knew the path took a sharp turn before entering the thickest part of the wood, and he stumbled on in the blackness, hoping that he would be able to negotiate the bend successfully by instinct

He was congratulating himself that he had done so when he came into violent contact with the wet trunk of a tree. The impact, startling in its suddenness and unexpectedness, knocked him breathless and for a second or two he leaned against the obstacle to recover.

He was considering the advisability of using his lighter to find his way back to the narrow track when he heard somebody speaking in an undertone, and recognized the voice as belonging to Gormley. He could not catch what the man was saying but the thin, cringing whine was unmistakable.

'You slimy little rat!' The rough angry voice that broke in was that of Dinsley. 'So that's your game — blackmail, eh? Who put you up to this — Baldock?'

Gormley's reply was inaudible, but whatever he said reduced Dinsley's hectoring tone to a mildness that was in startling contrast to his previous outburst.

'H'm! Well, we can't talk here . . . Come up to the house . . . '

There came the sound of squelching footsteps retreating and then silence. Chambers waited a moment or two before he took out his lighter and pressed the spring. The little glimmer was not a very satisfactory substitute for the torch but it was sufficient to show him the way back to the footpath.

His mind was full of the scrappy conversation he had overheard as be emerged from the footpath and skirted the Green towards his home. So the thin-faced Gormley, with his unctuous voice and obsequious manner, knew something about Dinsley and was trying to blackmail that dour and disagreeable man; knew something that was apparently known also to the stout, ill-mannered Baldock.

The sense of coming trouble that he had mentioned to Sergeant Akeman was obviously not entirely a product of his imagination. There was something queer going on.

He reached his little gate and had passed through when the sound of running footsteps came to his ears, and he paused inside, with his hand on the latch.

There was a street lamp a few yards away and as the runner came into the dim circle of light it threw, he saw that it was Ilene Dinsley. Her face was white and drawn and she was breathing with difficulty. A sob escaped her parted lips as she passed the gate and vanished into the rainy darkness in the direction of the High Street.

Oakley Chambers watched her until she was out of sight. What he had heard and seen that night justified his premonition, and he felt vaguely uneasy. The undercurrents seething below the peaceful surface life of the village which had given rise to that feeling of impending disaster he had experienced was gaining strength. For the ghosts of the past were mustering, gibbering and mouthing in preparation for the flood of fear and terror that was so soon to be loosed.

2

At the Wall Gate

Mr. Geoffrey Baldock was fond of proclaiming widely that he was a self-made man, thereby unconsciously denouncing himself as a bad craftsman. Short of stature, with a great deal more fat than was healthy for a man of his limited inches, his big, red, face was puffy and his nose squat and flattened. Above the coarse mouth with its thick lips lay a smear of ginger moustache, the colour of which was repeated in his thin brows and even thinner hair, which he brushed carefully in an unsuccessful effort to hide the incipient baldness about which he was very sensitive.

With a half-smoked cigar between his teeth he sat after dinner in his study, scowling at the fire and listening to the hiss and splash of the rain outside. There were people who inquired unkindly what use a study could be to a man who seldom read anything but the sporting papers and only wrote when it was necessary to put his signature to a cheque.

How this uncouth man had come by the money that had enabled him to buy West Lodge and settle down to a life of ease and leisure was a matter for speculation. That money was not lacking was evident, for the house was a large one and he maintained a considerable staff. It was generally supposed that he was a retired businessman, but what his business had been was a subject which Mr. Baldock refused to discuss, offering the vaguest of answers when anyone evinced curiosity in this direction.

He had come to West Dorling two years previously, unknown and unheralded, and was heartily disliked by the entire village, which resented his weekend parties, his surly manner, and the vulgar display that he made of his wealth.

He finished his cigar and flung the butt into the fire, and was in the act of pouring himself out a drink from the decanter of whisky that stood on a small table near his chair when the telephone bell rang. With a grunt of annoyance he got up.

'Hello!' he growled ungraciously, and then, as he recognized the caller's voice: 'Oh, it's you. What the hell do you want?'

The scowl on his face deepened as he listened to the reply.

'Well, you can't come here. What the devil's the matter . . . ? I won't! It's a filthy night! Can't you leave it till tomorrow . . . ? Oh, all right then. Come to the wall gate, I'll wait for you.'

He banged the telephone back on its rack angrily. What the devil did Dinsley want to see him for so urgently?

Still frowning, he moved over to the table, splashed whisky into a glass and gulped it down. Maybe it was a trap? His small eyes narrowed suspiciously, and going back to the desk he took a bunch of keys from his pocket, unlocked a drawer, and lifted out a heavy automatic. From the same drawer he took a clip of cartridges, slipped them into the butt and pulling back the jacket ensured that there was one in the breech. With his thumb he put on the safety catch and laid the

15

weapon down on the blotting pad. It was just as well to be prepared. Not that Dinsley would dare —

He helped himself to a cigar, bit off the end, and lit it, glancing at the clock as he did so. There was plenty of time. Dinsley couldn't get to the wall gate for another fifteen minutes at least

He crossed to the door, went out into the hall, and from the rack of coats and hats selected a mackintosh and a cap, which he carried back into the study. From a cupboard he took a pair of rubber overshoes, and sitting down in his chair laboriously pulled them on. Red-faced and breathing heavily from his exertions, he straightened up, puffed jerkily at his cigar for a minute or two, and then, rising to his feet, struggled into the mackintosh, put on the tweed cap, and going to the door, locked it. Picking up the automatic he dropped it into the right hand pocket of his raincoat and opened the French windows leading into the garden.

The rain was beating down as heavily as ever, and he grunted disgustedly at having to turn out on such a night. There was no help for it, however, and closing the window behind him he set off.

He had only gone a few yards before the cigar between his lips became a soggy mess of tobacco, and he flung it savagely away.

The wall gate lay at the end of a twisting path that wound through a mass of shrubbery. It opened onto a narrow lane, but it was seldom used except by Baldock himself, and usually kept locked. He reached it and, taking a key from his pocket, fumbled in the darkness. It turned silently, for the lock was well oiled, and reaching up he shot back the heavy bolt that also secured the door. Pulling the portal ajar, he waited for the arrival of his visitor.

It was several minutes before he came, and Baldock was growing impatient when a hurried footstep outside announced his arrival. The door was pushed further open and a dark figure slipped through.

'Are you there, Baldock?' The words were jerky and accompanied by heavy breathing, as though the newcomer had been hurrying.

'Of course I'm here!' snarled Baldock crossly. 'I've been here a hell of a long time! What's the idea, Dinsley, dragging me out on an infernal night like this?'

'Gormley!' panted Dinsley huskily. 'He knows!'

Baldock uttered an oath.

'What d'you mean?' he demanded harshly. 'How can he know?'

'I don't know how, but he knows,' said the other. 'He sent me a note this evening asking me to meet him in Longman's Spinney. I've only just left him. He wants a thousand pounds to keep his mouth shut!'

Baldock glared at his dimly-seen companion.

'How can he have found out?' he muttered. 'We've taken every precaution. Either you or Flood must have done something to make him suspicious!'

'Don't be a fool!' snapped Dinsley. 'Is it likely we should? I was wondering whether you hadn't put him up to it.'

'Me?' exclaimed Baldock roughly. 'What the hell do you take me for? Does Flood know?'

Dinsley shook his head.

'Not yet,' he answered. 'I tried to get him on the telephone before I rang you, but he was out. What are we to do, Baldock?'

'I don't know,' was the reply. 'This wants thinking about. I'll tell you what we're *not* going to do, and that is pay that little rat Gormley a thousand quid!'

'If we don't he'll talk,' muttered Dinsley uneasily.

'Will he?' snarled Baldock. 'He'll talk from Hell if he does!'

'You're not suggesting —' whispered the other.

'I'm not suggesting anything!' broke in his companion. 'But I'm not going to stand for having the 'black' put on me! D'you suppose it would end with a thousand? He'd come again for another thousand and then another. You ought to know what that sort of thing leads to. He'd suck us dry!' He paused. 'We'll have to see Flood about this,' he went on. 'How did you leave Gormley? Did you come to any arrangement?'

'I told him I'd have to consult you and

19

Flood,' said Dinsley, 'and he seemed satisfied about that.'

'Well, we can't see Flood tonight,' grunted Baldock. 'We'd better fix up a meeting for the morning, somewhere away from this place. We don't want to be seen together if we can help it. I'll tell you what — you know the old abbey at Claydon?'

Dinsley nodded.

'Well, we'll meet there at eleven o'clock tomorrow. Nobody ever goes near the ruins, and we can fix this thing up then. You get hold of Flood and tell him. Now clear off home. I'm going in before I catch my death of cold.'

He pushed his visitor towards the wall gate, and it was not until he had gone and the door locked and bolted that he relaxed his grip on the pistol in his pocket.

Mr. Baldock was a suspicious man and distrusted everybody. It would be a lucky thing for Dinsley and Flood if anything happened to him, just as it would be lucky for him if anything happened to them!

He came back to the comfort of his study, stripped his dripping coat, kicked off his goloshes, and helped himself to a drink.

So Gormley knew, did he? Well, he'd find his knowledge a dangerous possession. Perhaps Flood would be able to suggest a way of dealing with him. He knew what he would do, but Flood was more subtle. In the matter of subtlety the unpleasant and undersized Gormley was superior to any of them; but unfortunately for him, Mr. Baldock was destined never to discover this.

3

The Glass Arrow

Claydon Abbey, or what remains of it, lies half a mile to the east of the old Post Road that passes through the village of West Dorling and runs on to the small town of Middlethorpe. The road itself is in bad condition, many parts of it being impassable except on foot, for to suit the exigencies of modern traffic a new and expensive bypass has been constructed which cuts out the narrow streets of West Dorling and Claydon and joins the main thoroughfare again two miles beyond Middlethorpe at Lidbury.

The ruins themselves are practically invisible from the road. Thick under-growth and ivy has covered the crumbling stones, and where the monks were wont to tend their garden great trees have grown, obscuring the decaying work of their hands. There is a hint of an ancient cloister, the feel of paving beneath grass and moss, and from the twisting brambles rise stunted pillars which once towered aloft, supporting the arched roof of the central hall.

Perhaps because of the difficulty of finding the place, or more likely because it has no particular historical value and there is little to see, few people ever come near the ruins, leaving them to crumble in solitude to the dust which has long since been the fate of the earnest and industrious men who built the original edifice.

The rain of the previous night had ceased and a pale sun was struggling through the grey of the sky when John Dinsley came quickly along the old road and turned off by the lichen-stained milestone to make his way over the rough ground towards the meeting place. His harsh, lined face was troubled and the thick brows drawn together. He had succeeded in getting in touch with Preston Flood and arranging for the meeting this morning, but neither that nor his brief interview with Baldock had relieved his anxiety.

He came within sight of the abbey

ruins and paused, looking about for some sign of the other two, but the place was deserted. Evidently he was the first to arrive. Glancing at his watch he frowned. It was already past eleven.

Seating himself on a pile of stones, he took out his cigarette case and lit a cigarette. He had smoked half of it gloomily when he saw someone approaching and recognized the loud checked suit before he was able to distinguish the blotchy, red face of Mr. Baldock.

'Hello!' grunted that unpleasant man, ungraciously, as he came within speaking distance. 'Where's Flood?'

'He hasn't turned up yet,' answered Dinsley shortly.

'H'm!' Baldock, his short legs set wide apart, eyed the other unfavourably. 'Did you get in touch with him last night?'

'Of course I did!' snarled Dinsley irritably. 'D'you think I'd be here if I hadn't? I arranged this meeting and told him it was very urgent.'

'Perhaps something's happened to delay him,' muttered the other.

'Hope he doesn't keep us waiting long.

I want to get this business over and done with.'

'Not more than I do,' declared the other. 'I wonder how that little brute found out?'

'Does it matter?' snapped Baldock. 'All that matters is that he has found out, and we've got to find some way of keeping his mouth shut.'

'There's only one way that I can see.' Dinsley threw away his cigarette and rose to his feet. 'Other, that is, than agreeing to his demands.' He looked significantly at Baldock, and the red-faced man nodded.

'I agree with you,' he said. 'And I think Flood will, too.'

'What the devil's happened to him?' grumbled Dinsley, looking angrily at his watch again. 'It's twenty minutes past eleven already. Is he going to keep us waiting here all day?'

Baldock turned, and his small eyes scanned the portion of the old road that was visible from where he stood, but it was deserted.

'Well, he's either late or he isn't

coming,' he remarked. 'That's pretty obvious. What are we going to do?'

'What can we do, except wait!' retorted Dinsley. 'We can't settle this business without Flood. It's as much his affair as ours.'

'Supposing he doesn't come?' interrupted the other.

'He'll come,' said Dinsley with conviction. 'I couldn't say much over the phone, but he'll guess there was something serious.'

'Well, I hope he hurries up,' grunted Baldock shortly. 'I'm getting cold standin' about here.'

'There's no reason why we shouldn't wait in the cloisters,' said his companion, who was also feeling a little chilled. 'It's out of the wind and we can see just as well from there when Flood arrives.'

He stepped over a heap of broken masonry, and followed by Baldock made his way across the grass-grown flagstones beyond.

'That's better,' said Baldock. 'There was a hell of a wind out — '

He broke off, and his puffy, red face

went a curious grey.

'Look!' He gripped Dinsley's arm. 'What's that — over there by those brambles . . . ?'

The thin man looked and uttered a startled exclamation. Protruding from the confusion of brambles that grew at the base of the cloister wall was a foot.

'It's somebody fallen asleep, a tramp probably,' he muttered, and hurried forward with the alarmed Baldock at his heels.

A man lay on his back amid the trailing briars, his agonised face upturned, the moss and grass near him dappled red . . .

'My God!' whispered Baldock huskily, as he peered at the twisted face. 'It's Flood!'

Dinsley said nothing. He was staring with wide eyes at the thing that stood out from the dead man's breast and glistened in the dim, diffused light that filtered through the spreading branches overhead.

'An arrow!' he muttered almost inaudibly. 'An arrow of glass . . . '

Baldock's shaking fingers closed on his arm.

'Let's get away from here,' he breathed hoarsely. 'Don't stand there mumbling. For God's sake let's get away!'

Dinsley shook him off angrily:

'What's the matter with you?' he snarled. 'Pull yourself together, you fool!'

'Come away, I tell you,' whispered Baldock, his voice unrecognisable in his terror. 'Can't you see — when they find him — they'll say we did it — '

The calmer Dinsley eyed him suspiciously.

'I suppose you don't know anything about it?' he demanded accusingly.

'Me?' Baldock glared at him, his fear changing to sudden anger. 'What d'you mean? I wasn't even here. You was here first, if it comes to that — '

'When I saw you it might have been your second visit,' broke in Dinsley meaningfully.

'Look here,' blustered Baldock, his face flushing to a reddish purple. 'What are you trying to do, eh? Saddle me with your own crime? Is that it?'

'I didn't kill Flood,' said Dinsley curtly.

'Neither did I!' retorted Baldock. His

anger departed as swiftly as it had arisen, and he looked fearfully at the brambles which concealed the dead man. 'What's the use of stopping here arguing?' he muttered, licking his lips. 'Let's go before somebody sees us.'

He stumbled away, and Dinsley, with a backward glance over his shoulder, followed. They hurried over the rough ground to the old road and had scarcely disappeared from view round the bend when a man, who had lain concealed in the fork of a big tree near the ruins, began to descend from his precarious perch.

He reached the ground, stood for a moment listening, and then stole towards the ancient cloisters and peered down at the sprawling figure in the shadow of the wall. There was a queer expression on his wizened face when he presently turned away, and he chuckled once unpleasantly as he left the ruins.

Mr. Stephen Gormley had both heard and seen a great deal that morning which he thought was likely to prove very profitable to him in the future.

4

Trevor Lowe Is Interested

Mr. Trevor Lowe, that famous and popular dramatist, was a man with a great many friends; and it was not unnatural, therefore, that in the course of any given year he should receive a vast number of invitations. It was seldom, however, that he was able to find time to accept any of these numerous offers for his days were usually too fully occupied. Now and again, at rare intervals, he did manage to snatch a weekend, and it was during one of these exceptional holidays that he came in contact with the extraordinary business of West Dorling.

Tom Medlock had been chief crime reporter on one of the London dailies until illness had forced him reluctantly to give up his job. He had spent eighteen months in hospital and when he had come out, an invalid for life — he was suffering from an incurable disease — he was faced with a prospect that looked rather bleak. His state of health prohibited the strenuous life of a reporter and he had to seek a new means of livelihood. He took to writing articles, with an occasional short story, which provided him with the bare necessities of existence. And then he published a novel that met with instant success, wrote another which was even more successful, and on the proceeds bought a little cottage near Claydon.

In the days when he had been a crime reporter he had been one of Lowe's greatest friends. Criminology had been his hobby as well as his profession, and it was his habit to drop into the dramatist's flat in Portland Place at all sorts of odd hours for a drink and a chat.

Lowe had visited him several times while he was in hospital, and after the success of his book Medlock had repeatedly tried to persuade his friend to come down to the cottage at Claydon for a weekend. Again and again the dramatist had had to excuse himself, for the invitations had always coincided with an unusually heavy programme of work. At last, however, there had come a brief period of inactivity, and leaving Arnold White to look after anything that might turn up during his absence, Lowe had packed a bag and telephoned Medlock that he was coming down.

Tom had welcomed him effusively. His establishment was a bachelor one, run by an ex-naval seaman and his wife whom Medlock had met somewhere in his reporting days and remembered in the time of his prosperity. Although he called the house a cottage, it consisted of six bedrooms and three rooms on the ground floor, exclusive of kitchen and usual offices. Mrs. Jiffer, a buxom woman of fifty, attended to the cleaning and the cooking, and her husband looked after the garden and did such odd jobs as were necessary.

Lowe arrived on the Friday night, looking forward to a peaceful three days of congenial company.

'I'm afraid you'll find it a bit dull, old man,' said Medlock, when they had finished supper and were seated in his study. 'Life runs pretty evenly here. The only excitement we ever get is a rick fire or the arrest of a drunken labourer.'

'I don't know about the drunken labourer,' replied the dramatist, 'but you won't get any rick fires tonight. Listen to the rain.'

'According to the weather forecast,' said Tom, 'we're due for a fine spell. I hope we get it, for the country round here is worth seeing and it'll be a pity if you have to remain cooped up in the house all the time.'

'I shan't worry,' answered his friend, with a smile. 'I came to see you, Tom, not the country, and as far as dullness is concerned, well, I can do with a little. I've had a pretty exciting time recently.'

The ex-crime reporter eyed him a little enviously.

'I read about that business of the Bell Murders,' he said with a sigh. 'I miss the excitement sometimes. Still, I mustn't grumble.'

'How's the new book going?' asked Lowe, leaning contentedly back in his chair and puffing out clouds of smoke.

'Fairly well,' said his friend. 'To tell you the truth I'm a bit scared. The first two went so well that I'm afraid of having a flop with the third.'

'I don't see why you should,' remarked the dramatist. 'You've plenty of experiences to draw on, Tom.'

'Yes, that's true,' admitted Medlock, 'and I've found 'em darned useful.'

'I liked your first two books,' said Lowe. 'They rang truer than the ordinary crime stuff, which of course they should, seeing that you know more about crime and crooks than the average author.'

Tom Medlock chuckled.

'I should,' he said. 'I've spent half my life investigating one and mixing with the other. D'you remember the Borthwick's . . . ?'

He went on, stringing one reminiscence after another, and it was late when, after a final drink, he escorted his friend to bed.

The following morning after breakfast he suggested a walk, and since the weather was fine Lowe agreed readily. He soon discovered that Tom had not exaggerated when he described the country as worth seeing.

They walked slowly through winding lanes, chatting on a variety of subjects and enjoying the keen, sweet air, which was such a contrast to the petrol-laden atmosphere of London. Coming out on to a stretch of deserted road, Medlock paused.

'You ought to see our famous ruins,' he said, pointing across a waste of rough, gorse-covered ground to a distant wood. 'They're not really famous, but you ought to see 'em just the same.'

'You mean Claydon Abbey?' said the dramatist, and Tom looked a little surprised.

'Oh, you've heard of 'em, have you?' he asked, and when Lowe nodded: 'You're one of the few people outside the neighbourhood who has. They're not very well known.'

'You'd be surprised at the things I've heard of that are not very well known,' murmured Lowe. 'Produce your ruins, Tom, and let's inspect 'em.'

Medlock led the way over the uneven

ground that rose towards the fringe of trees that marked the beginning of the wood.

'The road we've just come from,' he explained, 'used to be the main thoroughfare until they built the bypass. Now nobody uses it, as you can tell by its condition.'

He knocked out his pipe on the handle of his stick, and pulling a pouch from his pocket began to refill it.

'We shall just have time,' he remarked, 'to look at the ruins and work back by Meadow Lark Lane to the house for lunch. Here you are, here's the beginning of 'em.'

He stabbed with the mouthpiece of his pipe towards a pile of grey stone that was half-concealed by ivy and rank grass.

'The cloisters is the best-preserved bit,' he went on. 'The rest is just heaps of masonry like this.'

'It's interesting to imagine the old monks at work,' said Lowe, looking about him. 'Can you visualize with what pride they must have dug the foundations and set the first stone? With what triumph they must have contemplated the finished result? With what scorn they would have treated anyone who had suggested that their labours were to end like — this?'

'The labours of all men shall come to dust and the work of their hands be as chaff before the winds of Heaven', quoted Tom.

He paused to light his pipe and the dramatist wandered on among the remains of the old abbey. Tom had struck a match and was cupping it in his hands to shield it from the wind when Lowe's voice called sharply.

'Medlock! Come here, will you?'

'What's up?'

The ex-reporter, puffing furiously to get the tobacco well alight, went in search of his friend. He found him standing over by the cloister wall.

'What have you discovered?' he asked with a smile. 'The long-lost treasure of the Ancient Order — ' And then, as he saw what Lowe was looking at, the smile froze on his lips. 'Holy smoke!' he breathed. 'Is he dead?'

The dramatist nodded.

'He's not only dead but he's been murdered!' he answered gravely. He pointed to the weapon that protruded from the dead man's chest, and Medlock gave a long, surprised whistle.

'An arrow!' he exclaimed incredulously. 'A glass arrow! By Jove, Lowe, what a story! Old Bishop would have gone wild with delight in the old days if I'd ever brought him anything like this!'

Lowe was ready to agree with him. Any normal news editor in Fleet Street would have hailed such an extraordinary crime with delight.

'It's incredible!' said Medlock excitedly. 'It's story-book stuff. It's not real!'

'It's real enough,' answered the dramatist. 'He was killed with the arrow.'

'I've heard of an arrow murder before,' said Tom, 'but not a glass arrow. Where in the world could the murderer have got it from?'

'That will be one of the chief lines of inquiry, unless I'm very much mistaken,' said Lowe. 'Look here, Tom, you'd better notify the police about this at once.'

'Who is the fellow?' said Medlock,

bending forward and screwing up his eyes, for he was a little short-sighted. 'Good God, it's Flood!'

'You know the man?' asked Lowe sharply.

'I don't know him personally,' answered the other, 'but I know him by sight. He lives just outside West Dorling, the next village to Claydon. What on earth was he doing here? And how did he come by his death?'

'That's for the police to find out,' said his friend. 'Go along to the nearest station and tell 'em, will you, there's a good fellow. You know this district better than I do.'

Medlock nodded.

'I wish I was still on the *Wire*,' he said wistfully. 'What a story!'

'Well, you may yet have a chance of a scoop,' retorted Lowe. 'You're the first on the field, anyhow.'

Medlock hurried away, and the dramatist, left alone, made a closer inspection of the dead man. The arrow was of clear, white glass, a little larger than a cigarette in circumference. The feathers at the butt end had been fused into the shaft and were not feathers at all in the actual sense of the word, but were constructed of something that looked like floss silk, but which Lowe decided was also glass very finely drawn.

So far as he could judge, the weapon had gone right through the man. He could not be certain of this, and until the police had seen the body he thought it best not to move it; but taking this supposition as correct he estimated the arrow's length to be a little over three feet.

It was an extraordinary weapon! So far as he could remember, unique. And likely to prove a valuable clue, for there could be very few in existence. What had made the killer choose such an unusual means of bringing about the death of his victim?

There was blood on the mixture of grass and moss on which the body lay, and he touched one of the stains with his finger. It was still tacky. The man had not, then, met his death so very long ago.

Almost mechanically he began to make an inspection of the immediate vicinity, but he found nothing. There were no traces visible on the grass-covered flagstones. Farther afield, however, he made a discovery that he thought might be important. Near a heap of masonry lay the remains of a cigarette. Two-thirds of it had been smoked but the end that had been thrown away bore the maker's name. It was a Balkan Sobranie, an expensive and unusual brand, and it was fresh and clean, proving that it had only been thrown there recently.

He put it back exactly where he had found it, preferring to point it out to the police when they arrived. He was intensely interested.

Surely there was some particular reason why such a peculiar weapon had been used? There were so many other means by which the murderer could have achieved his object. A knife or a pistol would have been far easier — and surer. Why had he chosen an arrow? And an arrow of such an unusual substance as glass?

He was still trying to find a satisfactory answer to this question when the police arrived.

5

Inspector Noyes Takes Charge

It would have been difficult to find a more appropriate name for Inspector Archibald Noyes than the one that his parents had bestowed upon him. His voice was a bellow, and even when he was not speaking he wheezed and grunted and made extraordinary sounds in his throat that were most disconcerting to those who were unused to these mannerisms.

He arrived in an ancient car that made as many weird noises as himself, and was accompanied by a bucolic constable and a slim, dark, good-looking man whom he introduced as Doctor Chambers.

'Glad to meet you, Mr. Lowe,' he boomed loudly. 'H'm! G-r-r! Of course I've heard of you. Hum! Ah! Yes! Mr. Medlock says Mr. Flood has been murdered. H'm!'

The dramatist nodded briefly, a little overwhelmed by this stupendous greeting, and explained how they had come to make the discovery.

The Inspector listened, keeping up a running commentary of hisses, grunts and growls. When Lowe had finished he went over to the body and bent down, peering at it, still hissing and spluttering.

'Ah! H'm! Queer business. Very queer business!' he roared. 'What do you make of this arrow, Mr. Lowe, eh? G-r-r!'

'I agree with you, it's a very queer business,' said the dramatist, suppressing an inclination to laugh.

Mr. Noyes scratched the side of his head with great vehemence, and nodded.

'You're right, sir. You're right!' he shouted. 'Ah! Ah! Hum! Have a look at him, Doctor, will you?'

Chambers, who had been standing silently by, moved over to the dead man and knelt beside the body. His examination was brief.

'He's quite dead,' he remarked, looking up. 'You don't need me to tell you that. The arrow pierced the heart and killed him instantly.'

'There's no doubt, I suppose, Doctor,'

put in Lowe, 'that it was the arrow which killed him?'

The doctor turned towards him quickly, surprise in his eyes.

'What exactly do you mean?' he asked.

'I mean,' said the dramatist, 'could he have been stabbed for instance, and the arrow inserted afterwards in the wound?'

The young doctor shook his head without hesitation.

'Quite impossible!' he declared with conviction. 'The arrow fits the wound exactly. There is not the slightest doubt, in my opinion, that it was the lethal weapon.'

'What made you ask that question, Mr. Lowe?' boomed the Inspector curiously. 'Had you any particular reason, eh? Uh?'

'Only this,' replied the dramatist, 'that if the arrow was the actual weapon of death it must have been shot from a bow. Which argues extraordinary skill in archery on the part of the murderer.'

'Not necessarily, old man,' put in Tom Medlock. 'He may have used the arrow as a dagger.'

The dramatist shook his head.

'No, Tom,' he answered. 'The force

44

required to drive it through the body would have snapped it. It's only glass, remember, and extremely brittle.'

'But surely,' protested the ex-reporter, 'that also applies to the bow idea?'

Again Lowe shook his head.

'No,' he said. 'Fired from a bow, the force would be level with the plane of flight. There would be no side stress, which would be unavoidable if the arrow had been used as you suggest.'

'Well, if you're right,' said Medlock, 'it's a valuable clue. There are not so many people nowadays who are experts in toxophily.'

'That's what I was thinking,' agreed Lowe. 'It narrows the field considerably.'

Inspector Noyes was interested.

'I see what you mean, sir,' he said. 'We've got to look for a fellow who's good at this archery business.'

'Exactly!' said the dramatist. 'The arrow itself should also be easily traceable. It's unique, so far as I know, and the workmanship is excellent. There should be no difficulty in discovering who made it.'

In this he was wrong. The maker of the arrows was never discovered, for he had been dead for over a century before the work of his skilful hand was used to cut short the life of Mr. Preston Flood.

The Inspector took a handkerchief from his pocket, and with difficulty withdrew the arrow from the wound. As he held it out for inspection Lowe saw that his rough estimate regarding its length had been nearly right. It was an inch or two longer than he had calculated.

The slender shaft was of solid glass, and the point was needle sharp. There was a notch in the butt to take the bowstring, and the whole thing was so fairy-like and delicate that it was almost impossible to believe it had been the means of taking a man's life.

Noyes sent the constable to fetch some paper from the car and, when he came back with it, carefully wrapped the weapon up.

'P'raps there'll be prints on this,' he boomed. 'Ah! G-r-r-! I'll have it examined at the station.'

'Do you know anyone in the district,' asked Lowe, 'who smokes Balkan Sobranie cigarettes?'

Out of the corner of his eye he saw Doctor Chambers give a slight start. Noyes shook his head.

'What are they, sir?' he inquired loudly. 'Some special brand?'

'They're not very common.' Lowe took him over to the place where he had found the end and pointed it out. 'I believe,' he went on, as the Inspector picked it up and stared at it, 'that Doctor Chambers can help us. You know of someone in the neighbourhood who smokes this particular brand, don't you?'

Chambers nodded.

'Yes,' he answered. 'I know of one person — John Dinsley.'

Medlock uttered a low whistle.

'Dinsley, eh?' he said. 'He was a friend of Flood's, wasn't he?'

★　★　★

The doctor shrugged his shoulders.

'Well, I don't know that you'd exactly

47

call him a friend,' he answered. 'They were acquainted but whenever they came in contact with each other they were always snarling and quarrelling.'

From the throat of Inspector Noyes came a series of strange and uncouth sounds.

'Well,' he bellowed, 'it looks very much as if Dinsley had been here this mornin'. This cigarette end is clean and dry, and the rain didn't stop till after seven.'

Lowe nodded. He had also noted that.

'Where does this man Dinsley live?' he inquired.

'Highfield House,' replied Chambers. 'On the outskirts of West Dorling.'

The Inspector carefully put the cigarette butt into an old envelope and stowed it away in his pocket.

'I think I'll have a word with Mr. Dinsley later,' he remarked. 'Always quarrelling, you say they were, Doctor?'

'Yes.' The young doctor hesitated, and Lowe was under the impression that he was considering whether he should say anything further. This impression was confirmed when he went on, after a slight pause: 'It's a curious thing, but I was only discussing these people with Sergeant Akeman last night.' He gave a brief account of his talk with the sergeant. 'You can call it a hunch or whatever you like,' he concluded, 'but I've been expecting something to happen for a long time.'

'Who's this man Baldock you mention?' inquired Lowe.

'A surly brute,' answered the doctor. 'A cross between an ex-pugilist and a bookie. Plenty of money and lives in a nice house not far from Dinsley. I don't know whether it's got anything to do with this affair, but going through Longman's Spinney on my way home from the police station last night, I accidentally overheard a rather curious conversation between Dinsley and an unpleasant little beast called Steve Gormley.'

He related what he had heard, and the Inspector and Lowe listened interestedly.

'It's quite possible it may have a distinct bearing,' commented the dramatist. 'These three men were acquainted, and one of them was being blackmailed. Since Dinsley mentioned the name of

Baldock to this man Gormley it seems quite likely that they were all mixed up in it. How long have they lived in the district?'

'They were here when I came,' answered Chambers, 'and I've been here just over a year.'

'Did they all come together?' said Lowe.

The doctor shook his head.

'No,' he replied. 'They came within a few months of each other.'

The dramatist pursed his lips. His holiday had accidentally brought him into contact with a crime that appealed strongly to his imagination. Here were three men who had apparently taken up their residence in the district within a short while of each other. One of them had been killed in circumstances that were decidedly unusual, and the other was being blackmailed for something which apparently was known to at least one of the others. He took the Inspector aside.

'I have no official standing, of course,' he said in a low voice, 'and I don't want to butt in on your business. But I must confess that I am very curious about this affair, and I should like to watch events.'

Noyes emitted a startling series of grunts and throaty gurgles.

'Pleased to have any help you can give me, Mr. Lowe,' he answered. 'Bit of a puzzle at present, eh? Though it looks very much to me as if this man Dinsley was the feller.'

'It certainly looks as if he was here this morning,' admitted Lowe cautiously. 'But whether he killed Flood or not is another matter. He may be able to account for the presence of that cigarette end.'

'Well, we shall see,' boomed the Inspector. 'I don't think there's much more we can do here. I'll leave the constable on guard, arrange for the photographers to come along and photograph the body and then we'd better notify the household concerning the man's death. Do you know where Mr. Flood lived?' he called loudly across to Chambers, who was chatting in a low voice to Medlock.

'The Hermitage,' answered the doctor. 'It's a fairly big place on the hillside, not far from Lord Hillingdon's estate.'

'Any family?' asked Noyes, and Chambers shook his head.

'No. He was supposed to be a bachelor,' he answered.

'H'm! Ah! G-r-r-! Well, we'll get along,' said the Inspector. 'You stay here, Radley, until they come to take the body away.'

The bucolic policeman nodded, and from the expression on his ruddy face did not altogether relish the task.

'You coming with me, sir?' said the Inspector, looking at Lowe.

'I should like to,' answered the dramatist, and then, realizing that he could scarcely desert his friend in this cavalier fashion, turned to Medlock. 'You don't mind?' he asked, and the ex-reporter shook his head.

'No,' he replied. 'You carry on. I'm going back to the house to get in touch with old Bishop.

Lowe saw the sparkle in his eyes and, guessing the cause, smiled.

'Going to have a final fling, Tom?' he said, and Medlock nodded.

'I'm going to see if they'll let me cover this business,' he answered. 'It's the biggest thing I've ever come up against and it'll make a fitting 'swan song.' If you're going to West Dorling,' he added, 'perhaps Inspector Noyes would drop me at the bottom of Rook Lane. It'll save me a walk.'

The Inspector readily agreed, and leaving the constable in charge they made their way over the rough ground to the little car. It was a tight squeeze for the four of them, but they managed it, and Noyes sent the decrepit machine bumping protestingly along the old road.

They dropped Medlock where he had asked, and left Doctor Chambers at the gate of his little house by the Green. At West Dorling's rural police station the Inspector halted to notify the astonished Sergeant Akeman of what had taken place, to telephone to Middlethorpe for an ambulance, and to send the police photographers to the ruins.

'Now, sir,' he said when he rejoined Lowe, who had waited in the car, 'we'll go along to the Hermitage and see if there's anything useful to be learned at the dead man's house.'

6

The Empty Safe

The Hermitage was a medium-sized house, pleasantly sited on the rising slope of a wooded hillside. It was approached by means of a winding lane into which the drive gates opened, and as the Inspector turned the car into the short, shrubbery-lined avenue that led up to the porch, Lowe caught a glimpse through the surrounding trees of trim lawns and colourful flowerbeds. There was a wide gravel space in front of the main entrance and here Noyes brought the little machine to a squeaking stop.

He got out, followed by the dramatist, and then ascended the shallow steps to the front door. There was a bell-push let into the brickwork at the right-hand side, and to this the Inspector applied his thumb. After a few seconds' delay the door was opened by a thin, dark, man in the conventional garb of an upper servant, who surveyed them a trifle superciliously.

'Mr. Preston Flood live here?' inquired Noyes loudly.

The butler inclined his smooth head.

'Yes, sir,' he replied. 'But he is not in at the moment.'

'I should like a few words with you,' said the Inspector curtly. 'I'm Inspector Noyes from Middlethorpe.'

Lowe saw an expression of surprise cross the thin features of the servant — surprise mingled with a trace of alarm.

'What is your business, sir?' he inquired a little more respectfully.

'I can't discuss that on the doorstep,' said Noyes. 'Can we come in?'

Rather reluctantly, the butler stood aside and they entered the comfortably furnished hall.

'Now,' began Noyes, as the butler closed the door, 'what's your name?'

'Tresler, sir,' replied the servant.

'You say your employer is not in?' continued the Inspector. 'What time did he go out?'

The butler hesitated.

'May I ask the reason for these inquiries?' he said doubtfully. 'Has anything happened to Mr. Flood?'

'Why should you think that?' demanded Noyes sharply.

The servant made a deprecating gesture.

'I can think of no other reason for a police visit,' he answered.

'Well, you're right,' said the Inspector. 'I'm sorry to inform you Mr. Flood is dead!'

'Dead!' The butler was startled. His dark face paled and he glanced quickly from one to the other.

'He was murdered some time during this morning in the ruins of Claydon Abbey,' said Noyes. 'And I'm here to make inquiries concerning his movements.'

The servant was genuinely shocked. He put up a hand to his lips and his voice, when he spoke, was uncertain.

'Murdered!' he repeated. 'I — I don't understand — '

'We none of us understand at the moment,' boomed the Inspector. 'When did you last see Mr. Flood?'

'This morning, at breakfast,' answered the shaken man. 'How — how did it happen — '

'What time would that be?' interrupted Noyes, ignoring his question.

'Eight o'clock,' said the butler promptly. 'Mr. Flood always had breakfast at that hour; he was most particular.'

'And that was the last time you saw him?'

The man nodded.

'Yes, sir,' he replied. 'I heard him go out, but I didn't see him.' He hesitated a moment and then added: 'He had two telephone calls. I mention the fact, because it was unusual.'

'Oh, he had two telephone calls, did he?' The Inspector was interested. 'We'll check those up. What time would it be when you heard him go out?'

'It was between a quarter to nine and nine,' said Tresler. 'I can't be sure of the exact time.'

'That's near enough,' grunted Noyes. 'I understand that your master was friendly with a Mr. John Dinsley, and also a Mr.

Baldock, both living in the neighbour-hood. Is that correct?'

For the first time the man smiled.

'No, sir, I should hardly call it correct,' he replied. 'Mr. Flood knew both Mr. Baldock and Mr. Dinsley slightly, but I wouldn't say he was friendly with them.'

'What would you say then?' put in Trevor Lowe.

'Well sir, both the gentlemen men-tioned called here once and there was a proper row between them. You could hear it all over the house.'

'When was this?' asked the dramatist.

Tresler screwed up his face in an effort of memory.

'A long time ago, sir,' he answered at last. 'More than a year, I think. I know neither of them have been since.'

'When did Mr. Flood come to live here?' inquired Lowe, while Inspector Noyes wheezed and grunted in the background.

'Eighteen months ago,' answered the man.

'And were the other two here then, living in the district?' the dramatist went on. 'Or did they come later?'

'Mr. Baldock was here, sir,' said the butler. 'Mr. Dinsley came about a month after, I believe.'

'Were you in the employ of Mr. Flood before, or did you come to him when he bought this house?'

'I came to him when he bought this house,' replied Tresler. 'I was sent down by an agency in London.'

'What sort of a man was Mr. Flood?' said Lowe, and the butler pursed his thin lips.

'Well, sir,' he answered reluctantly, 'it's difficult for me to say. He wasn't a — a gentleman, if you understand what I mean. I've been employed by some of the best people in the land and — well, Mr. Flood gave me the impression that he wasn't quite used to this style of living.'

'I see,' murmured Lowe, nodding slowly.

The butler's words had confirmed the judgment he had already formed from the dead man's appearance. In spite of the immaculate clothes and the expensive linen, there had been a coarseness about the features which had led him to the conclusion that Mr. Preston Flood was not of the class which usually occupies a pretentious house in the country.

'What sort of men are these other two?' he continued, after a pause. 'Baldock and Dinsley?'

'Mr. Dinsley's a gentleman,' said the butler without hesitation, 'but Mr. Baldock — ' He shrugged his shoulders expressively. 'Well, Mr. Flood wasn't what you'd call 'polished' but Mr. Baldock is just East End.'

Inspector Noyes was making sundry sounds in his throat which Lowe took to be a sign of impatience. He turned towards him.

'Sorry to interrupt, Inspector,' he apologized.

'All right, Mr. Lowe. All right,' grunted Noyes. 'I just wanted to put one more question, that's all. Have you noticed any difference in Mr. Flood's behaviour recently?'

'How do you mean, sir?' asked the butler.

'I mean,' said the Inspector, 'has he

appeared upset, or worried?'

'Well, he did appear to be a little ill-tempered at breakfast,' said Tresler, 'but he was often like that, so I didn't really attach much importance to it.'

'That,' put in Lowe quickly, 'would be after the two telephone calls?'

The man nodded.

'H'm! Ah!' The Inspector fired a broadside of guttural noises. 'Well, I don't think I want to ask you anything further at the moment. We shall take charge of the house, of course, and I should like to have a look through the dead man's effects.'

'And we might begin with the study,' suggested the dramatist. 'Where is it?'

'I'll show you, sir,' said the butler, and he led the way across the hall to a closed door on the right.

Opening this, he stood aside to allow them to pass into the room beyond. It was a big room, comfortably furnished and with some taste. One wall was covered by book shelves, containing a variety of novels which Lowe saw consisted, for the most part, of crime and detective stories. A thick carpet covered the floor, and in the centre of the room was a large pedestal desk. Several leather-covered chairs were grouped round the big fireplace, and this constituted the bulk of the furniture, with the notable exception of a large safe which stood against the wall behind the door.

Noyes glanced about him keenly.

'We might run through the desk, Mr. Lowe,' he said, and turned to the waiting butler. 'All right. If we want you we'll ring for you.'

The man departed reluctantly and, from the expression of his face, rather disappointed that he had not been allowed to remain to watch their activities. When he had gone Lowe shut the door and the Inspector produced a bunch of keys which he had taken from the body, and after one or two unsuccessful attempts he discovered the one that fitted the drawers of the desk. He unlocked them, and with the dramatist's help ran through the contents.

There were several bills, mostly from local tradesmen; a file of receipts; and a quantity of headed paper and envelopes, but nothing of any importance. No letters, bank book, or anything that was calculated to throw a light on Mr. Flood's mysterious death.

'I should think the safe is the most likely place to contain the kind of information we're seeking,' said Lowe, when they had exhausted the desk. 'Have you got the key for that?'

The Inspector examined the bunch.

'This looks like it,' he said, and walking over tried it in the lock. 'Wrong one,' he said disappointedly, and tried another, with the same result. One after the other he went through the bunch, but none of the keys fitted. 'Queer,' he muttered. 'Surely he'd have kept his safe key on him.'

'There were no other keys?' asked Lowe, and Noyes shook his head.

'No, only this bunch,' he answered. 'You saw what I took from his pocket, I wonder where he'd be likely to keep it?'

He went back to the desk and began to rummage through the drawers in case he had overlooked the key. He was still searching when an exclamation from the dramatist made him look up.

Lowe had gone over to the safe and gripped the handle, and under his hand the heavy door swung open.

'Wasn't it locked — ' began Noyes, coming to his side.

Lowe shook his head.

'No,' he answered grimly, 'and that's why you couldn't find the key. The person who killed Flood took it and came here after the murder and opened the safe. Look, it's empty!'

7

Mr. Dinsley's Alibi

The Inspector peered into the bare interior of the safe with a frowning face, and it needed only one glance to confirm Lowe's statement. There was nothing in it. It was as empty as when it had come from the makers. He straightened up with a perfect barrage of weird noises to signify his astonishment.

'Peculiar, isn't it?' murmured the dramatist.

'Peculiar, sir!' roared the Inspector. 'I should say it was. It's a licker, that's what it is! Fancy the feller who killed Flood having the nerve to come here in broad daylight and clear out the safe.'

'I agree with you,' said Lowe thoughtfully. 'It wanted nerve. But that's obviously what he did. That's why you couldn't find the key on that bunch. He took it.'

He crossed over to the French windows, which opened into the garden, and examined the fastenings. They were unlatched, and on the brass catch he found a bright scratch, evidently made by a knife inserted in the space where they met. He pointed this discovery out to the Inspector, and that still-astonished man grunted.

'He came from the back, you see,' said Lowe, 'and probably went the same way. Ring for the butler, will you?'

Noyes looked about him, saw a bell-push near the fireplace, and going over pressed it.

'There's just a possible chance,' went on the dramatist, 'that one of the servants may have seen this man — if it was a man,' he added.

'You're not suggesting that it might be a woman?' said the Inspector, and Lowe shrugged his shoulders.

'There's nothing to show it wasn't,' he answered. 'A woman could have fired that arrow as easily as a man. We've nothing at present to indicate the sex of the killer.'

'Only the cigarette end — ' began Noyes.

Lowe smiled.

'Women smoke nowadays almost as much as men,' he interrupted. 'Don't count too much on the cigarette end, Inspector. It doesn't say because Dinsley smokes Balkan Sobranies it was necessarily he who was at the ruins this morning. They're not difficult to obtain at any reputable tobacconists.'

The Inspector had opened his mouth to reply when there came a tap at the door and Tresler entered.

'Did you ring?' he asked, and Lowe nodded.

'Yes,' he said. 'Have you any idea what that safe contained?'

The man looked quickly towards the open door and his face changed.

'It's empty!' he gasped.

'We can see that,' growled Noyes. 'What we want to know is, did Mr. Flood keep anything of value in it?'

'I don't know what was in it,' answered the butler. 'I remember seeing it open once when I came in unexpectedly, and Mr. Flood was putting some papers away. It was about half-full then.'

'Was your master in the habit of

keeping money there?' inquired the dramatist, and Tresler shook his head.

'I couldn't say, sir,' he answered. 'I only saw the safe open once.'

'Are you aware,' continued Lowe, 'whether he usually kept the key on this bunch?' He picked up the keys, which Noyes had left on the desk.

Tresler came a few steps nearer and looked at them.

'Yes sir,' he replied. 'I remember seeing that bunch hanging from the lock on the occasion I mentioned.'

The Inspector shot a quick glance at Lowe.

'That's that,' he said.

The servant looked from one to the other curiously.

'Has there been a robbery?' he asked.

'I'm inclined to think there has,' said the dramatist. 'What other servants are employed here?'

'Two maids, the cook, and the chauffeur,' said the man promptly. 'There's also a gardener and a boy, but they don't live on the premises.'

'Have either of the maids been in this

room this morning?'

'Not since it was cleaned first thing,' answered Tresler. 'Mr. Flood always liked this room tidied as early as possible so that he wouldn't have to be disturbed.'

'We are of the opinion,' said Lowe, 'that the safe was opened by your master's own key after he had been killed. From indications on the latch of these windows we believe the person who opened the safe came across the garden. Did you see or hear anyone during the morning?'

Tresler, whose eyes had opened wide, shook his head.

'No, sir, I heard nothing,' he replied. 'If I had I should have mentioned it.'

'Where would the other servants be?' asked the dramatist.

'Upstairs, sir, doing the bedrooms,' answered the butler at once. 'That is, of course, the maids. The cook was in the kitchen preparing lunch and the chauffeur was in the garage cleaning the car.'

'Is it possible to overlook the garden from the garage?' said the dramatist,

'No, sir,' said Tresler, shaking his head. 'I don't think the maids could have seen or heard anything, either. If they had they would have reported it to me.'

'Fetch them, anyhow,' said the dramatist, 'and the others as well.'

The butler departed, and he had barely gone when they heard the sound of voices in the hall, and in a few seconds he returned.

'Excuse me, sir,' he said, 'are you Mr. Lowe?'

The dramatist nodded.

'There's a gentleman wants to see you,' went on the servant. 'A Mr. Medlock — '

'Oh, yes,' interrupted Lowe quickly. 'Ask him to come in, will you?'

Tom Medlock's face was wreathed in smiles when he entered.

'I guessed you'd be here,' he said, 'so I got out my car and came along on the off-chance. It's all right. I've been on to Bishop. Once more I'm a fully-fledged reporter!'

'Congratulations,' said Lowe, but Inspector Noyes looked a little dubious.

'I hope you won't go printing anything without the permission of the police, sir,' he said uneasily.

'You needn't worry, Inspector,' put in Lowe. 'Mr. Medlock has had too much experience to do that. I think you'll find him of inestimable help in getting to the bottom of this business.'

'Thanks for the testimonial,' said Medlock. 'Have you got hold of anything yet?'

The dramatist told him of the discovery they had made concerning the safe, and he pursed his lips.

'Extraordinary!' he muttered. 'Pretty risky thing to do in broad daylight. He must have had a strong reason for wanting to get hold of the contents of the safe before anyone saw them.'

'Yes,' agreed Lowe, 'and the most peculiar thing is that he took *everything*. If he'd been after one particular document it would be more understandable. But he hasn't left anything.' He broke off. 'Here are the servants,' he said, as there came a shuffling of feet outside. 'Perhaps we shall learn something from them.'

Two frightened girls and a stockily-built man in leggings were shepherded into the room by Tresler.

'The cook and the gardeners will be here in a few minutes, sir,' said the butler, as Lowe surveyed the little group.

The chauffeur was in his shirtsleeves, his hands black with oil and grease. The two maids were typical country girls, both scared and curious about the ordeal that had been suddenly inflicted on them.

They answered the questions, however, which Lowe and the Inspector put to them without hesitation. Neither of them had seen or heard anything. They had been busy all the morning cleaning the bedrooms in the upper part of the house, and on such occasions as they had looked through any of the windows the garden had been deserted. The chauffeur, whose name was Wilks, was no more informative. Mr. Flood had ordered the car for two o'clock that afternoon. It had been his intention to go to London, and he was most particular that the machine should be speckless. The chauffeur had spent the entire morning polishing and cleaning, which meant that he hadn't stirred from the garage.

Lowe had just put a final question to

the man when the cook and the gardeners arrived. The former had been in the kitchen from which it was impossible to see any more of the garage than a small courtyard, for a high yew hedge shut off the kitchen quarters. Neither could the elderly gardener and his youthful assistant supply any useful information. They had been at work in the shrubbery near the drive gates and had seen no one. Lowe dismissed the servants and turned to the Inspector and Medlock.

'There's nothing to be gained from them,' he said disappointedly. 'The person who emptied that safe came and went unseen. I think our next move is to interview Dinsley.'

The Inspector nodded.

'I'll just get on to the telephone exchange first, sir,' he remarked, 'and see if I can trace those two calls.'

He picked up the receiver as he finished speaking and presently was connected with the supervisor. After giving his name and stating what he wished to know, he waited, a large hand over the mouthpiece.

'It shouldn't take them long,' he said. 'The exchange at Middlethorpe doesn't handle many calls, and they ought to be able to find them easily. Hullo! Yes!' He removed his hand and bellowed into the instrument. 'There's no doubt of that . . . ? Thank you.' He slammed the telephone down on its rack and turned to the others with a curious expression. 'The first call,' he said, 'was from Dinsley.'

'Oh, was it,' said the dramatist. 'Dinsley again, eh?'

'Yes,' said Noyes. 'I'm beginning to think, Mr. Lowe, this is going to be easier than we thought.'

'Don't be too optimistic, Inspector,' warned Lowe. 'The fact that Dinsley put through a telephone call to Flood this morning doesn't necessarily mean that he killed him.'

'No,' admitted the Inspector. 'But taken in conjunction with the cigarette end you must agree it's peculiar. Flood would hardly have been at the ruins at all unless some appointment had been made, and this call from Dinsley seems to suggest that's what it was for.'

'What about the other call?' asked Lowe.

'The other call,' said Noyes slowly, 'was from a public box in the village.'

'Was that the one after Dinsley's?' asked the dramatist.

The Inspector nodded.

'I'd like to know,' murmured Lowe, 'who put through that second call. In my opinion that's the more important of the two.'

'It's going to be difficult to find out,' said Noyes dubiously, 'unless he was seen entering or leaving the box.' He turned to the telephone again. 'I'll just ring up the station and arrange for a constable to be sent here, and then we'll go along and see what Mr. Dinsley has to say.'

He got on to Sergeant Akeman, made his arrangements, and rang for Tresler.

'We're leaving here now,' he said, when the butler put in an appearance, 'but a man will be coming up to take charge. I'm locking this room and taking the key. Nobody is to be admitted to the house under any pretext whatever. You understand?'

The butler nodded in silence. Noyes closed and latched the French windows, and when they had passed out into the hall, locked the study door and put the key in his pocket.

'Now,' he said, when they had taken their places in the little car, 'how do we get to this place of Dinsley's?'

Neither Lowe nor Medlock could tell him.

'You'd better ask the way from someone in the village,' suggested the dramatist.

'Highfield House, wasn't it?' said Noyes, and Lowe nodded.

The Inspector sent the little car speeding down the drive, and when they reached the High Street pulled up before a tiny shop that sold tobacco and papers. He disappeared within, returning after a second or two with the information he wanted.

'Straight ahead,' he said, 'and it's a few yards beyond the crossroads.'

They found it easily, an imposing entrance between brick pillars, with ugly wrought iron gates that stood open, revealing a well-kept gravel drive beyond. The house itself was visible as they turned into the approach, a more pretentious place than Flood's, but less picturesque. As they came to a stop by the front door Lowe caught a glimpse of a girl's yellow jumper and a tweed skirt flitting through the pillars of a long pergola. He concluded she must be the daughter Doctor Chambers had mentioned, who had gone running past his house on the night when he had overheard the conversation between Dinsley and Gormley in Longman's Spinney.

A trim maid came in answer to their ring, and Inspector Noyes inquired if Dinsley was at home.

'Yes, sir,' said the girl. 'But he's very busy; I don't think he can see anyone.'

'I think he'll see me,' roared the Inspector, and he gave his name.

The maid looked a little startled, but she said nothing, and closing the door disappeared. After a short interval she was back again. 'Mr. Dinsley will see you, sir,' she said. 'This way, please.'

She ushered them into a spacious hall

and led the way over to a partly-open door on the left. Inspector Noyes was the first to cross the threshold, and Dinsley, who was sitting in a big chair by the fireless grate, dropped the newspaper he had been reading and looked up quickly.

'Inspector Noyes?' he inquired. 'What do you wish to see me about?'

The Inspector advanced a few paces, followed by Lowe and Mediock. As Dinsley caught sight of his companions his eyebrows drew together.

'Who are these people?' he demanded testily.

'They are working in conjunction with me, sir,' said Noyes. 'I understand you were acquainted with Mr. Flood, of the Hermitage.'

'Yes, I know him.' The grey man's eyes flickered from one to the other restlessly. 'Why do you say 'were acquainted'? Has anything happened to him?'

'Yes, sir,' answered Noyes. 'Mr. Flood was found murdered among the ruins of Claydon Abbey this morning.'

'Good God!' Dinsley sat up with a startled expression. 'Are you serious?'

'It's hardly a matter I should joke about!' retorted the Inspector indignantly.

'Dear, dear, what a dreadful thing!' The man hoisted his gaunt length out of the chair and stood up, his thin face moving from side to side. 'I wasn't exactly a friend of Flood's — in fact we didn't hit it off — but I'm very sorry to hear this. How did it happen?'

'He was killed in rather a peculiar way, sir,' said Noyes. 'Death was due to a glass arrow which had pierced his heart.'

The man before him stared in astonishment.

'A glass arrow?' he repeated. 'How extraordinary!'

Lowe, who was watching him keenly, thought that his astonishment was a little overdone.

'Dreadful! Dreadful!' he continued. 'But why have you come to me? I know nothing about Flood or his private affairs.'

'We came to you, sir,' said the Inspector, 'for two reasons. The first of which is because I am informed by the telephone exchange that you put through a call to Mr. Flood's house this morning.'

79

'Oh, I see.' Dinsley was a little disconcerted. 'Yes, that's quite right, I did.'

'Can you tell me for what reason?' asked Noyes.

'Well, I could,' answered the grey man hesitantly, 'but I really don't see — ' He broke off and shrugged his shoulders. 'Oh, well, there's no reason why I shouldn't,' he went on. 'I hold some shares which Flood was anxious to purchase. I had no particular wish to sell them and I told him so. But he was very anxious and asked me to think it over. I arranged to let him know this morning, and I did.'

'I see,' said the Inspector. 'You didn't arrange to meet Mr. Flood at the ruins?'

'Good Heavens, no!' said Dinsley quickly. 'What put that idea into your head?'

'I'm given to understand, sir,' said Noyes, 'that you habitually smoke a brand of cigarettes called Balkan Sobranies.'

Dinsley raised his eyebrows, and Lowe thought a flicker of apprehension came into his eyes.

'Yes, I do. What's that got to do with it?' he answered.

80

'A partly-smoked Balkan Sobranie was found among the ruins,' explained the Inspector. 'It must have been dropped there after the rain stopped this morning, which was at seven o'clock.'

'Oh, I see.' The grey man drew in his breath sharply. 'And you are under the impression that I dropped it. Well, you're wrong, Inspector. And I should like to point out that I'm not the only person in the world who smokes Balkan Sobranie cigarettes.'

'No, sir,' said Noyes. 'Naturally I'm aware of that. All the same it's an unusual brand and I should be glad if you would tell me whether you've been out this morning?'

The shaggy grey eyebrows drew together.

'Really,' exclaimed Dinsley angrily, 'that question strikes me as a little impertinent, Inspector.'

'I'm sorry if you should look at it in that way, sir,' said Noyes. 'But I'm afraid I must repeat it all the same.'

'Well, if you really want to know,' snapped Dinsley, 'I have been out. I spent the morning with Mr. Geoffrey Baldock.'

'At his house?' inquired Noyes.

Dinsley shook his head.

'No!' he retorted. 'We went for a walk.'

'Did you go near the ruins?' inquired Lowe.

'We did not go near the ruins,' he said. 'We walked through Bexley Wood, which, if you're acquainted with the district, you will be aware is in the opposite direction.'

'I presume,' continued the dramatist, 'that Mr. Baldock will bear out your statement?'

'I've no doubt he will if you ask him,' answered Dinsley. 'If you're under the impression that I know anything about the death of this man Flood you're mistaken.'

'We're not suggesting that you do,' said Lowe calmly. 'But you must realize, Mr. Dinsley, that in a case of murder every inquiry that is likely to throw a light on the crime is necessary.'

'I shall not dispute your statement, sir,' said Dinsley stiffly, 'although I have no idea who you are.'

'My name is Lowe,' murmured the

dramatist. 'Trevor Lowe.'

Dinsley started. Evidently the name was familiar to him. His thin lips opened, but before he could speak the words that were plainly hovering on his tongue the telephone bell broke into a shrill clamour. The instrument stood on a low bookcase beside the chair on which he had been sitting; and turning, he lifted the receiver.

'Hello!' he called, and then: 'Yes, he's here. Hold on a minute, will you?' He turned to Inspector Noyes. 'You're wanted by Sergeant Akeman,' he said, and the Inspector uttered an exclamation.

'Excuse me,' he muttered, and took the telephone from Dinsley.

'What is it?' he barked. 'Noyes speaking.' There followed a short silence during which they heard the faint chatter of an excited voice come from the instrument. 'What?' The Inspector shouted the word, and on his face appeared an expression of incredulous wonder. 'All right, I'll go straight along. Yes, at once.' He turned and stared at them, the telephone still in his hand. 'I'm afraid, sir,' he said, letting his eyes rest on Dinsley, 'that Mr. Baldock will not be able to bear out your statement.'

'Why? What do you mean?' snapped the grey man.

'Mr. Baldock has just been found dead!' answered Noyes gravely. 'One of the servants discovered him ten minutes ago near a gate at the end of his garden. He was quite dead and had obviously been murdered.'

Lowe's voice was harsh when he spoke. 'How was he killed?' he asked.

The Inspector swallowed and looked at him queerly.

'Same as Flood,' he answered. 'By a glass arrow!'

8

The Second Crime

A sound came from Dinsley, a queer, half-strangled gasp, and the dramatist saw that his face was the colour of dirty putty.

'My God, it's not true!' he whispered hoarsely. 'It's not true — it can't be true! I only left him half an hour ago — '

'I'm afraid it is true, sir,' boomed the Inspector. 'Mr. Baldock's butler rang up the police station a few minutes ago, and Sergeant Akeman, who knew I was coming here, got in touch with me immediately.'

The man raised a shaking hand to his lips.

'Dead!' he muttered. 'First Flood and now Baldock — ' His voice was scarcely audible, and in his eyes was a look of fear.

'I shall have to postpone further questions for the time being, sir,' said the Inspector. 'I must go straight along to Mr. Baldock's house at once.'

'Yes, yes, of course!' Dinsley nodded mechanically, but he seemed scarcely to understand. 'I — I — ' He hesitated, muttered unintelligibly and continued: 'This has been a great shock to me. It's terrible — ' He finished incoherently, and there was no doubt that he was speaking the truth, though the nature of the shock, in Lowe's opinion, was not entirely due to surprise and horror at the death of an acquaintance. It was something much more personal. It was inspired by terror. In that revealing moment when Noyes had broken the news that had come over the telephone Dinsley had suddenly become conscious of his own danger.

That's how Lowe read the expression that had come into the man's face at any rate. There was something that connected these three men; something in which they were all concerned, and two of them had been killed by an unknown hand. In the twitching grey face and trembling lips the dramatist saw panic — the panic inspired by the belief that he might be the next.

Inspector Noyes inquired the way to

Baldock's house, and Dinsley, with an effort, pulled himself together and jerkily supplied the necessary directions. On the way to the car Medlock gripped his friend's arm.

'Did you see his face?' he whispered. 'When the news came through?'

The dramatist nodded.

'He was scared to death,' said the reporter with conviction. 'Genuinely scared. Flood's death didn't upset him half so much.'

'No, I noticed that,' murmured Lowe. 'And I can guess the reason.'

'He's frightened out of his wits,' said Medlock. 'Terrified that the arrow killer will have a go at him.'

'I think you're right,' agreed Lowe.

They reached the car, and Noyes turned a worried face towards them as they were about to get in.

'I don't know whether I oughtn't to get someone to keep an eye on that feller,' he remarked, jerking his head towards the house. 'Baldock's death has destroyed his alibi and — ' He broke off as a girl came hurriedly round the corner of the building.

It was the girl in the yellow jumper and tweed skirt whom Lowe had seen earlier, and she was breathing heavily, as though she had been running.

'You're — you're the police, aren't you?' she asked, as she came up to the car.

'Yes, Miss,' said the astonished Noyes. 'What — '

'You've been to see my father, haven't you?' she broke in, speaking rapidly and unevenly, her eyes moving nervously from one to the other. Lowe thought she might have been pretty but for her extreme pallor and the drawn look which made her face appear almost haggard.

'Yes,' began the Inspector again, and again she interrupted him.

'I thought you had,' she said. 'They told me you had — the servants. What have you been to see him about?'

The big eyes were frightened, the bloodless lips quivered, and she plucked with restless fingers at a woollen tassel which ornamented the front of her jumper.

'We came to ask your father a few questions, Miss Dinsley,' said Lowe. 'A friend of his, Mr. Preston Flood, was murdered this morning, and — '

'Mr. Flood — murdered!' She turned towards him at the sound of his voice, and to his surprise there was relief in her face. 'Oh, was that why you came? I — I thought — I wondered — ' She stammered and stopped abruptly.

'What did you wonder?' asked the dramatist gently.

'I — I — ' a tinge of colour came into her pale cheeks, and she looked embarrassed. 'It was nothing. When was Mr. Flood killed?'

'This morning, Miss,' said Inspector Noyes, his loud voice emerging from a series of throaty rumbles. 'He was shot with a glass arrow — '

She uttered a startled, inarticulate little cry, and the momentary colour receded from her face, leaving it white, even the lips.

'No! Oh, no!' she breathed. 'You don't mean that? You can't mean that!'

'It's quite true,' said Lowe. 'Mr. Flood was killed with a glass arrow, and so, we have just learned, was Mr. Baldock.'

'Mr. Baldock? Geoffrey Baldock?' Ilene Dinsley's eyes were wide, and in their blue depths lurked a fear unbelievable. 'I tell you it's impossible! It *must* be impossible!'

'Why do you say that?' asked the dramatist curiously, for the flabbergasted Inspector was incapable of speech, beyond even being able to make his usual commentary of hisses and grunts. He could only stare at the girl in abject astonishment.

'I — I — ' She pulled herself together with an effort. 'I — oh, don't take any notice of me. I didn't mean anything. It gave me a shock, that's all.'

She turned suddenly, and before any of them could say anything further hurried away.

'Well!' gasped the Inspector, finding his voice. 'What d'you make of that?'

'Curious, wasn't it?' murmured Lowe, his brows drawn together.

'Curious?' grunted the bewildered Noyes. 'D'you think she's batty?'

The dramatist shook his head.

'No,' he answered. 'I think she was

under the impression that we'd come to see her father about something else altogether. When she heard Flood had been murdered she was relieved, until you mentioned he'd been killed by a glass arrow, and then,' — he paused — 'and then, for some reason best known to herself,' he added slowly, 'she was terrified.'

'Why?' demanded the Inspector.

Lowe shrugged his shoulders.

'You don't expect me to answer that, do you?' he said, with a little one-sided smile. 'I know no more than you do why.'

'Because,' suggested Medlock, 'she associates a glass arrow with something or someone.'

'Probably,' agreed the dramatist. 'It was the glass arrow that scared her, anyway.'

'I think we'd better have a word with her later,' said Noyes. 'It seems to me she may know a lot. It's my belief she thinks her father committed these murders, and that's why she's so frightened. I'm sending up a man straight away to keep an eye on Mr. Dinsley.'

'I think you're wise,' agreed Lowe.

They drove to the little police station, and found Sergeant Akeman in a state of unusual excitement.

'Two murders in one morning!' he said. 'And the doctor was only saying to me last night that nothing ever happened round here.'

'Have you notified Doctor Chambers?' said the Inspector curtly.

'Yes, sir,' said the sergeant. 'He's gone straight up to West Lodge, and I've sent a constable up as well. They'll be waiting for you when you get there.'

'Can you get hold of another man?' asked the Inspector.

'Yes, sir,' answered Akeman. 'Flinders has just come in.'

'Send him up to Dinsley's house,' ordered Noyes. 'Send him right away. Tell him to keep an eye on the place and to notify you if Dinsley tries to leave.'

Akeman's eyes widened behind his spectacles.

'Blimey!' he exclaimed. 'You don't think it was Dinsley who did those two fellers in, do you?'

'Never mind what I think,' growled

Noyes. 'Do what I tell you.'

He left the wondering sergeant to carry out his instructions and went back to the car, accompanied by Lowe and the reporter.

West Lodge was not very far away from Dinsley's house. It lay at the end of a private road which turned off the High Street. They were admitted by a frightened-looking butler and found a constable and Doctor Chambers waiting in the hall.

'My premonition seems to have come true with a vengeance,' said the doctor, with a rather mirthless smile.

'It does!' grunted the Inspector. 'Have you seen the body?'

Chambers shook his head.

'No, not yet,' he answered. 'I waited for you.'

Noyes turned to the agitated servant.

'Are you the butler?' he demanded.

The man nodded.

'What's your name?'

'Holford, sir,' was the tremulous answer.

'It was you who made the discovery and rang up the police station, wasn't it?'

went on the Inspector, and again the servant nodded. 'Well, tell us, Holford, how you came to find Mr. Baldock.'

The butler licked his dry lips.

'The master came home, sir,' he began, 'about half-past twelve. He wasn't in a very good temper, and he slammed off into his study. I had occasion a little later to consult him about a bill. I knocked on the door of the study and when there was no reply I went in. Mr. Baldock was no longer there, but the French window leading into the garden was open. I thought perhaps he'd gone for a stroll, which he sometimes did, and I went to see if I could find him.' He hesitated. 'I found him,' he went on, in a lower voice, 'near the wall gate. He was lying on his face and there was blood on the path. Something thin and shiny was sticking out from his back, a glass thing, shaped like an arrow. I — I touched his hand and it was limp, and he didn't move, and then I ran back to the study and telephoned the police station.'

'You didn't move him at all?' said Noyes.

'No, sir,' replied the butler, taking a handkerchief from his pocket with a shaking hand and wiping his damp face. 'No, sir. I only just touched his hand.'

'Was the wall gate open?' asked the Inspector, but Holford was unable to tell him. He had not waited long enough.

'H'm!' grunted Noyes. 'All! G-r-r-! Take us to the place where you found your master.'

The butler led the way across the hall, opened a door, and ushered them into a room that was furnished like a comfortable office. Lowe noticed the absence of books, and guessed that Mr. Baldock's leanings were not towards literature. The French windows, which opened on to a shrubbery-lined path, were ajar, and they followed Holford through and along a twisting track. A hundred and fifty yards from the house it turned abruptly, and they caught a glimpse of a high wall in which was set a green painted gate. Near the gate, on the gravel path, lay the crumpled figure of a man, face downwards, his outstretched hands curved so that the fingers appeared to be clawing at the ground before him.

'There you are, sir,' whispered the butler hoarsely, and pointed.

From Inspector Noyes' throat came a succession of grunts and wheezes. He approached the body and stared down at it.

A rather loud checked suit showed up in vivid contrast to the dull yellow of the gravel path, and from between the broad shoulder blades projected the slender glass shaft of an arrow — an exact replica of the weapon which had killed Preston Flood. There was a dark stain where it entered the cloth of the jacket, and a pool of blood had oozed from under the body and soaked into the path.

Lowe and Medlock looked down at the dead man with grave faces, although there was a tinge of excitement in the reporter's eyes. For some seconds Inspector Noyes stood in silence, his eyes taking in every detail. Then he turned to Chambers.

'All right, Doctor,' he said curtly.

The young police surgeon stepped forward, knelt beside the body, and made a quick examination.

'He hasn't been dead very long,' he said, looking up. 'About an hour, I think.'

'You sure of that?' asked the Inspector.

'Well, not within twenty minutes either way,' he answered. 'That's impossible. Do you want me to remove the weapon?'

Noyes nodded.

'Yes,' he said. 'Be careful, though. Use your handkerchief.'

The doctor had some difficulty, but eventually he succeeded, and holding the arrow in his handkerchief passed it to the Inspector, who took it, and after a glance leant it carefully against the wall near the gate. When he came back Chambers had turned the dead man over.

The red face wore an expression of surprise, and the thick lips were open slightly as though he had been in the act of uttering a cry when death had come to him. Chambers pointed to a stain on the front of the waistcoat.

'The arrow went right through him,' he said. 'From the amount of blood I should say it severed one of the larger blood vessels.'

Lowe, who had been watching in silence, suddenly turned to the white-faced butler and pointed towards a coppice of trees that backed the shrubbery.

'Is that private property?' he asked.

The man shook his head.

'No, sir,' he answered. 'It's a little wood that runs through to the main road.'

The Inspector looked round curiously.

'Why did you ask that, Mr. Lowe?' he inquired.

'Because, in my opinion,' said the dramatist, 'that's where the arrow was fired from. Baldock was standing here by the gate, with his back to the wood, and the murderer loosed the arrow from a branch of one of those trees.'

The Inspector surveyed the trees with a frown.

'What makes you think that?' he grunted.

'It's pretty obvious, surely,' replied Lowe, and he proceeded to explain. 'The weapon entered the back in a downward direction, which means that it began its flight from a height considerably above Baldock's head. If you visualise him standing here where he fell and take a rough line level with the angle of the arrow shaft you'll see that it ends mid-way up those trees. You agree, Tom?'

Medlock nodded.

'The murderer climbed one of these trees,' said Lowe, 'and when Baldock presented a suitable target fired.'

'How did he know Baldock was coming here?' demanded Noyes, and the dramatist shrugged his shoulders.

'Perhaps we shall discover that,' he said. 'But evidently he did. It's hardly likely he would have waited on the off-chance. I think you can be certain that he made sure of Baldock's presence near the wall gate before he lay in wait with his bow and arrow.'

'"Who killed cock robin",' murmured Medlock, but there was no humour in his voice.

'Exactly!' said Lowe softly. '"Who killed cock robin. I, said the sparrow, with my bow and arrow".'

'"Who saw him die"?' grunted Medlock. 'It's a pity we can't complete the rhyme and find the 'fly with his little eye'.'

The dramatist smiled grimly.

'It is only on very rare occasions that you get an eye witness to a murder,' he remarked. 'Still, maybe we shall be able to trap our sparrow yet. Is this door often used?' He addressed the last part of his remark to the scared butler.

'No, sir,' answered the man, shaking his head. 'It's usually kept locked and bolted. The tradesmen come to the other side of the house.'

Inspector Noyes had returned to the body and was busy going through the pockets of the dead man's clothing. Lowe strolled over to the narrow door and examined it. After a moment or two he stretched out his hand, gripped the latch, and pulled. The door swung open.

'Unlocked and unbolted,' he said, turning to Medlock. 'That's suggestive.'

'Of what?' asked the reporter.

'According to Holford,' said Lowe, 'the door was seldom used. It was kept fastened. This morning it's unfastened. It seems only reasonable to suppose that Baldock unfastened it. Therefore he came to keep an appointment with somebody

100

who he expected to arrive by way of the wall gate.'

'Yes, I see what you mean,' Medlock nodded. 'Which argues that the murderer was known to him.'

'I don't think there's any doubt that the murderer was known to both of them,' said the dramatist thoughtfully. 'Though whether they looked upon him as a possible killer is another matter. I'm inclined to think they didn't.'

'Why?' demanded his friend.

'Because of Dinsley's attitude,' said Lowe. 'Dinsley's scared. He's scared because he thinks he may share the same fate as Baldock and Flood. But he's scared of the unknown. He hasn't any idea who it is who is going about shooting up his friends with glass arrows. Neither, which is both a peculiar and an interesting point, does the glass arrow suggest anyone to his mind.'

'It suggested something to that girl,' muttered the reporter. 'If she's not crazy the mention of the arrow gave her a pretty bad shock.'

'Yes.' The dramatist rubbed his chin

and stared at the slim weapon that rested against the wall. 'Yes, that's something worth remembering, Tom. It suggested nothing to her father but it did to his daughter. Something that was particularly horrible, to judge by the effect it had on her.'

He lapsed into a thoughtful silence, which was broken by the loud voice of Noyes.

'Well, that's that!' bellowed the Inspector, scrambling to his feet, his face red from his exertions. 'There's nothing in his pockets except the ordinary things you'd expect to find.'

'What did you think there might be?' inquired Lowe, rousing himself from his reverie.

Noyes shrugged his shoulders.

'I don't know,' he answered. 'I thought there might be a note or something. I heard what you said about the door, Mr. Lowe, and I agree with you. He came here to keep an appointment with someone.'

'Dinsley,' put in Medlock.

'Oh, you think so, too, do you, Mr.

Medlock?' The Inspector nodded. 'That's what I think. In my opinion Dinsley killed Flood and then, after clearing out the safe, came up here and did this fellow in.'

'You may be right,' said Lowe, 'but you'll have difficulty in proving it.'

'Why?' demanded the Inspector. 'He had plenty of time. He was out all the morning.'

'Oh, I grant you the time,' said the dramatist. 'But you've forgotten the choice of weapons. I tell you quite frankly, Inspector, that only an expert in archery could have killed either of these two men, and you've got to prove that Dinsley was such an expert.'

'Well, for all we know he may be,' argued Noyes, hissing and grunting. 'What is there against that?'

'Nothing at all,' said Lowe. 'I'm not saying that Dinsley's guilt isn't possible. All I'm saying is that you've got to prove he could have committed the crime.'

'Well, the death of Baldock leaves him without an alibi,' said the Inspector. 'I'm pretty sure, in my own mind, that Dinsley's the man, the more so after the

103

queer behaviour of his daughter. I believe she knows he's guilty and that's what made her carry on like she did.'

Lowe said nothing. He was not at all sure that he agreed with Inspector Noyes over the reason for the girl's strange behaviour.

The Inspector looked across at the waiting Holford.

'Now,' he said, 'can you suggest any reason why your master should have come to this gate?'

The man began to shake his head, and then hesitated.

'No, sir,' he answered slowly, 'unless it was the telephone call.'

'What's that?' asked Lowe sharply, turning quickly towards him.

'I heard the telephone bell ring, sir, soon after he came in,' explained the butler.

The dramatist glanced meaningfully at Noyes.

'Flood had a telephone call, too,' he remarked.

'From Dinsley!' snapped the Inspector. 'If this call was from Dinsley, too, I think we've got him. Will you wait here with the body, Doctor? I'll send the constable down when I get back to the house.'

Chambers nodded, and picking up the arrow gingerly by its extreme tip Noyes set off up the path back to the house. Reaching the study, he rested the weapon carefully against one wall and picked up the receiver of the telephone. In a few seconds he was speaking to the supervisor of the Middlethorpe exchange. He put practically the same questions he had put earlier that morning, and his face was disappointed when, after a short delay, he received his reply.

'The call wasn't from Dinsley,' he remarked, as he dropped the instrument back on its rack. 'It came from a call box in the village.'

'The same call box from which Flood was rung up,' murmured Lowe. 'If you can find the mysterious caller, Inspector, I think you've got the murderer.'

9

Mr. Dinsley is Afraid

John Dinsley stood staring at the empty grate for some time after his visitors had left him. His face was still pale and his hands twitched spasmodically — the outward and visible sign of the inward terror that was gripping at his soul.

Presently he turned, walked over to the decanter that stood on a side table, and poured himself out a generous supply of whisky, which he gulped down neat. The spirit brought a faint tinge of colour back to his sallow cheeks.

He shivered. But for the fear that possessed him he would have had no regrets. The death of the two men made a considerable difference to his income. It augmented it by two thirds, and in ordinary circumstances this would have been a gratifying outlook. The shadow, however, which rested heavily upon him, prohibited any elation or even satisfaction.

Baldock and Flood had died violently, and Dinsley wondered fearfully whether the fate that had overtaken them would reach out towards him. And there was also Gormley to be dealt with. What difference would this make to the demands of the unpleasant little man? Gormley knew! In some extraordinary way he had surmised the secret, which had been shared by the three of thcm, and his knowledge was a menace — a menace that he would now have to deal with alone.

He began to pace the room, gnawing viciously at his lower lip. The situation was unpleasant and dangerous, and the danger threatened from three different sources. He was under no illusions concerning the reason for the police visit that morning. They suspected him — what a fool he had been to leave such a palpable clue as that cigarette end about — and they had not been satisfied with the answers he had given to their questions. Baldock, with whom he had arranged his alibi, could no longer substantiate it, and anything approaching police inquiries was going to be awkward.

Of the three dangers, however, this was the least. Gormley was infinitely more serious, and the other, the unknown, most serious of all. Who had been responsible for the deaths of Baldock and Flood?

The name of the most likely person flitted through his mind, but he shook his head as he dismissed the possibility. It couldn't be he! It wouldn't be he. He hated them enough, it was true, and if there had been any advantage to be gained Dinsley could quite imagine he would have been prepared to resort to murder. But there wasn't. On the contrary, their deaths would leave him in a worse position than ever. Then, who was this unknown who killed with such a strange weapon?

He came to a halt by the window and stared moodily out. He was shaken to the very core — fearful for the present, terrified of the future . . .

The faint sound made by the opening door caused him to swing round in alarm.

'Who — ' he began, and then, as he saw it was his daughter who had entered:

'What do you want? I'm very busy.'

'Is it true,' she asked, 'that Mr. Baldock and Mr. Flood have been killed?'

'What concern is it of yours?' he snapped angrily. 'Clear out of here, can't you?'

But she made no movement to obey the harsh order.

'Killed — with a glass arrow,' she murmured, staring at him, her face the colour of chalk. 'Is that right?'

'How do you know? Who told you?' he demanded roughly.

'Those men who were here this morning,' she answered, and with an oath he gripped her wrist with such force that she winced.

'You've been talking to them!' he accused. 'What have you been saying? What did they ask you?'

'You're hurting me!' she said, and he let her go with a muttered apology. 'They didn't say anything to me. I asked them why they'd come to see you, and they told me.'

'Well, what are you looking so scared about?' he grunted. 'You never liked

Flood and Baldock, so it shouldn't matter to you whether they are alive or dead.'

'I — it gave me a shock,' she murmured, mechanically rubbing her bruised wrist. 'It was the arrow — ' She stopped with a little shiver, and he eyed her suspiciously.

'What do you know about the arrow?' he said sharply. 'Why should the fact that they were killed by an arrow give you a shock?'

She moistened her lips.

'I — I don't know,' she stammered. 'There's — there's something horrible about it.'

'You're lying!' He came closer and glared down into her frightened eyes. 'You're lying, Ilene! What do you know about the arrow? Tell me!'

He caught her by the shoulders and gave her a little shake.

'You're lying, I tell you!' he repeated. 'The glass arrow means something to you. What?'

'Let me go!' She wrenched herself free. 'I know nothing about it. I tell you I know nothing about it!' The words came hurriedly and hoarsely, and with a sob she turned and stumbled from the room.

Dinsley made a movement as if to check her, and then, shrugging his shoulders, gave up the attempt and stood staring at the closed door through which she had made her exit.

What had upset the girl? Something, that was evident. She knew something. He frowned and bit his lip. What significance had the fact that Flood and Baldock had been killed with a glass arrow for his daughter? She was obviously panic-stricken. Well, he could question her later. In her present state it was useless, but she knew something, and he'd get it out of her sooner or later.

Once more he began his patrol of the apartment, trying desperately to collect his thoughts and force his mind to follow a coherent line. He found it difficult. They strayed from the police to Gormley, to the unknown menace that had already destroyed his two companions and might, at any moment, destroy him. Who was responsible for the murders? Who, among all the people they had come in contact with, was the most likely to be behind the killings?

And strangely enough, as he attempted to make his mental catalogue of the many persons in whom he and the two dead men had aroused an enmity sufficient to warrant such a terrible retribution, the one name that should have been splashed across his mind in letters of fire never occurred to him.

For John Dinsley had forgotten a certain episode that had happened many years before — an episode in which he and the two dead men had been the prime movers. And perhaps there was a reason why his memory failed him, for the name that should have come instantly to his mind was the name of a dead man who had died in the mud and blood of Flanders and been buried in a nameless grave . . .

★ ★ ★

Mr. Stephen Gormley read through the letter he had with much thought and labour just finished writing and shook his narrow head. He was an unpleasant and repulsive-looking man. His thin, stringy neck rose out of a grimy collar that appeared to be several sizes too large, his ears protruded bat-like from each side of his almost bald cranium, and together with his small eyes and large jutting nose this gave him the appearance of some prehistoric reptile. His pendulous lower lip prevented his mouth from completely closing, so that it was always possible to see the few broken and discoloured teeth, and when, as now, he was thoughtful, the tip of his tongue.

He had, at one period of his life, been a lawyer's clerk, but circumstances and Mr. Gormley's unfortunate predilection for acquiring other people's property without their consent, had reduced him to his present state. An unenviable one, for he existed precariously by picking up such crumbs as came his way.

Seated in the plain chair in the barely-furnished little bed-sitting room, which he occupied at Mrs. Bole's small cottage on the outskirts of West Dorling, he read the letter through for the second time, and after long consideration tore it up into microscopic pieces. Getting up, he carried these carefully to the tiny grate and burned them, watching eagerly to see that no scraps remained undestroyed. He would not write; he would wait for a suitable opportunity for a personal interview; it was safer. His early legal training had made him cautious of committing anything to writing.

He came back to his chair, searched in the ragged pockets of his clothing, and produced a cheap packet of cigarettes. Lighting one of the three that remained, he lay back and surveyed the situation. Fate and his own acuteness had placed in his hands the chance of making a good deal of money. That this necessitated blackmail worried him not at all, for Mr. Gormley had existed for a long time on judicious blackmail, but never on such a large scale as he now contemplated. With care he ought to clear enough money to enable him to live in comfort for the rest of his days. With Flood dead it would rest with Dinsley and Baldock, but that would make no difference; they would have to pay. The secret that he had stumbled on involved them all equally, and his silence was just as necessary to the two as it had been to the three.

He had come straight back from the ruined abbey after witnessing the tragedy of the morning, and was not yet aware that Baldock need no longer be taken into consideration in his scheme. Had he been so aware, however, it would not have troubled him. There was still Dinsley, and — the other.

He rubbed his thin hands complacently. The other was going to be of considerable profit, but he required handling more carefully.

Mr. Gormley, from his point of vantage in the tree, had seen the fate that had overtaken Preston Flood and realized that in crossing the man who killed him he was dealing with a dangerous personality.

He would have to take steps to safeguard himself thoroughly before approaching him, and it was this that was occupying his mind at the moment.

Mr. Gormley decided that his plans must be thoroughly perfected before he showed his hand. It should not be difficult. A statement setting down the exact facts could be lodged somewhere in conditions that would ensure it being opened at his death. A word to this effect to the man he was dealing with would render him completely safe from physical violence, and then he could sit back in comfort and even luxury, living on the double income which he would draw.

He had asked Dinsley for a thousand in the first instance, but on thinking the matter over he came to the conclusion that this was an inadequate sum, and multiplied it by five. Five thousand from Dinsley and five thousand from the other.

His little eyes glittered greedily. A sum sufficient to cover all his modest wants. He was not a man who believed in display and ostentation. A little cottage, good food and clothing and a sufficient surplus to enable him to satisfy his few luxurious tastes was all he required. And this was within his reach. He held these people in the hollow of his hand; could send Dinsley and his associate to prison with a word. Could send that other to the trap!

He drew the cheap pad of paper towards him on which he had previously written the letter, dipped his pen into the bottle of ink and began to write, carefully and methodically, his eye-witness account of the murder of Preston Flood . . .

10

Trevor Lowe Makes a Suggestion

Trevor Lowe sat in Inspector Noyes' small office at Middlethorpe police station and surveyed that puzzled individual thoughtfully.

Tom Medlock had gone to telephone the news of the latest tragedy to the *Daily Wire*, and they were alone.

'I don't mind admitting, sir,' grunted the Inspector, 'that I can't make head or tail of it. The thing that beats me is why these glass arrows were used. Why didn't the murderer choose an easier weapon?'

'You're asking me something that I can't tell you,' answered the dramatist, shaking his head. 'I've no more idea than you. But there must be something significant in the choice of the arrow.'

'But what can it stand for?' demanded Noyes, wrinkling his brows and emitting a series of rattles in his throat. 'Can you guess that?'

Lowe shook his head again.

'No, I'm afraid I can't,' he said.

''It certainly had significance for that girl,' muttered the Inspector, drawing meaningless little lines on the blotting pad in front of him with a pencil. 'It gave her a pretty bad shock when she heard how these men had been killed. I still believe,' he went on, as Lowe made no comment, 'that Dinsley's at the bottom of this business.'

'I think he knows something,' agreed the dramatist, 'but I don't think he was responsible for the deaths of Flood and Baldock. The news of Baldock's death was evidently a shock to him.'

'Well, you may be right,' said Noyes, 'but I've put a man on to watch him, all the same.'

'You're wise there,' said Lowe, nodding. 'I think Dinsley ought to be closely guarded from now on.'

'You're not suggesting that Dinsley is in any danger?'

'I should think it was quite probable,'

119

answered the other, eyeing him steadily. 'Listen, Noyes. There's very little doubt, so far as I can see, that Dinsley, Flood and Baldock were closely associated. All this business of their not being friendly is so much bunkum, in my opinion. And there's less doubt that their association was not entirely an innocent one. You remember what Doctor Chambers overheard in the wood?'

'About Gormley, you mean?' said Noyes, and Lowe nodded.

'Yes,' he went on. 'This fellow Gormley evidently knows something, and he was trying to extract money to keep his mouth shut. That is definite. What Chambers overheard could only mean blackmail. In fact Dinsley accused him of blackmail, and seemed to be under the impression that Baldock had put him up to it.'

'Which doesn't agree with your idea that Baldock, Flood, and Dinsley were in some underhand practice together,' argued the Inspector. 'Baldock would hardly be likely to spoil his own scheme by providing an outsider with the means of blackmailing him.'

'No,' said the dramatist. 'And we've no evidence that he did.'

'Dinsley evidently thought so,' grunted Noyes. He flung down his pencil and shrugged his shoulders. 'It's all a mix-up, Mr. Lowe,' he growled angrily. 'And we seem to have arrived at a deadlock. There's no doubt that your suggestion was right, and that the arrow that killed Baldock was fired from one of those trees in the wood at the end of the garden. When we examined the place we found sufficient traces to confirm that. But who fired it, and why, we are no nearer discovering. There's no prints on the arrows themselves, and unless we can get that girl to talk, or Dinsley, I don't see what more we can do.'

'The girl may be able to tell you something,' said Lowe. 'But I don't think Dinsley knows. He's scared, naturally, since his two associates have been murdered, and he's afraid that he may suffer the same fate. But he doesn't know why they were murdered or who murdered them, that I'm convinced.' He took out his pipe and began to fill it slowly.

'However, there are plenty of lines of inquiry to follow. The most obvious is to try and trace the origin of the arrows. They're unique. I've never seen anything like them before. The workmanship appears to me to be foreign. This man who used them must have got them from somewhere, and it shouldn't be difficult to discover where. Once we do that it's possible it'll provide a clue to the killer.'

'I'm getting on to that this afternoon,' grunted Noyes. 'I believe we'll have to have the Yard in this before we've finished, Mr. Lowe. I'm certain the Chief Constable 'ull insist on calling 'em in when I make my report.'

'I think you'd be wise if you asked for assistance,' said the dramatist. 'I'm not suggesting for one moment, Inspector, that you're not capable of handling the affair, but you haven't the facilities.'

'I agree with you, sir,' said Noyes. 'This is a big thing, and I'm willing to admit that I don't feel inclined to take the responsibility of handling it on my own. Anyway, the inquiry concerning the origin of the arrows will have to go to London.'

'Yes.' Lowe struck a match and applied it to the bowl of his pipe. 'There's another thing that might go to London with advantage,' he continued, when the tobacco was well alight. 'I suggest that you take the fingerprints of the two dead men and send them up to Records.'

'Do you think we might get results?' asked Noyes quickly.

'I think it's very probable,' answered the dramatist, blowing out a cloud of smoke and watching it thoughtfully. 'In my opinion these men were undoubtedly crooks, and therefore it is not unreasonable to suppose that they may, at some period of their lives, have been in prison. In which case there'll be a record.'

'Yes, I think your idea is good, sir,' said Noyes, and he made a note on the pad at his elbow.

'It would be interesting to find out,' Lowe continued, 'what brought them all to West Dorling. They're not the type of men who would settle down in the country for sheer love of it. They were here for a purpose, and they all came more or less together.'

'I'm wondering,' said Noyes, scratching his chin, 'whether it wouldn't be a good move to detain Dinsley on suspicion.'

Lowe shook his head quickly.

'I think it would be a stupid thing to do,' he answered. 'You've really no case against Dinsley, and therefore you couldn't hold him for long. Apart from which, while he's at large he may do something that will provide us with a clue.'

'There's something in that,' agreed the Inspector, and looked at his watch. 'I must go and see the coroner's officer and arrange for the inquest,' he went on, rising to his feet. 'What are you going to do, sir?'

'I'm going back to Mr. Medlock,' answered the dramatist. 'I shall be there all the afternoon if you want me. If there's anything I can do don't hesitate to let me know.'

'That's very good of you, and I'm very grateful for your assistance,' said the Inspector sincerely.

'In the meanwhile,' said Lowe, as they walked across the charge room, 'you might let me know if anything further turns up.'

'You can depend on that, sir,' said

Noyes. '*If* anything turns up,' he added dubiously.

Lowe left him at the corner of the street and turned in the direction of Medlock's cottage. It was some distance, but he elected to walk sooner than take advantage of the Inspector's suggestion that one of his men should drive him home. The gentle exercise stimulated his brain, and he wanted to think over the events of the morning

It was not the murders that intrigued him so much as the choice of weapons. Why had the murderer used such an extraordinary means of killing his victims? It was by no means easy to use a bow and arrow, that was with any degree of certainty, and yet in both cases the shaft had flown straight to its mark. It argued that the wielder of the bow was an expert in archery, which, in itself, was uncommon. In these days few people were interested in toxophily.

He decided that it would not be a bad idea to write to the Secretary of the Toxophilite Society and ask for a list of members. There was just the possibility that it might yield results.

Medlock had just come in when he reached the cottage, and Mrs. Jiffer was laying the table for a belated luncheon.

'It's lucky you're only 'avin' somethin' cold,' she commented severely, 'otherwise it 'ud 'ave been spoiled.'

'We shall be glad of anything,' said Medlock. 'At least, I shall; I'm ravenous. Old Bishop is wild with delight, Lowe,' he went on. 'They're making a front page splash. He says it's the most picturesque murder that's ever come his way.'

The dramatist smiled at his friend's outburst of enthusiasm.

'It's certainly the most unusual,' he admitted. 'The glass arrow lifts it into a class of its own.'

'That's what got Bishop,' said Tom. 'He says it's the answer to a news editor's prayer. What happened after I left?'

'Nothing much,' answered his friend. 'Noyes, who, by the way is a particularly capable officer, is setting one or two inquiries on foot which may lead to something.'

'Oh, well, we don't want it to end too soon,' said the reporter. 'The public likes suspense. You can't give 'em too much of it so long, of course, as you keep the interest going.' He pulled up a chair and sat down at the table as Mrs. Jiffer entered with a dish of particularly appetising-looking ham, flanked by an enormous bowl of salad. 'What's the programme for this afternoon?'

'There isn't one,' said the dramatist. 'So far as I can see very little else can be done until after the inquest, or Noyes gets some replies to the inquiries he has started.'

Medlock pursed his lips.

'I should like a good follow-up for the *Wire*,' he remarked, and Lowe laughed.

'I'm afraid we can't butcher anybody else to make a reporter's holiday,' he misquoted, helping himself to salad. 'You'll have to be content to wait until the inquest for your next sensation, Tom.'

His prophecy was not justified. Before the inquest could be held a third tragedy took place — a tragedy so unexpected and so apparently divorced from the main issue that it was not until much later that they realized how closely it was connected with the other crimes.

11

Lord Hillingdon Hears the News

Dorling Manor is sited on the slope of a wooded hillside. Its broad acres of pastureland spread out fan-shaped at the end of its terraced garden, which drops in a series of giant steps to the wood which circles the foot of the hill. It is a rambling old mansion of grey-white stone, softened here and there with patches of ivy and creeper.

In the old days, when the village of West Dorling consisted mainly of scattered farms and labourers' cottages, the 'Big House', as it was called, supplied the local point of interest, for it provided the livelihood of the majority of the villagers. Even now it was still looked upon as the most important part of the village, and the present Lord Hillingdon was treated with something of the respect and awe due to a feudal baron.

The tenth earl was an old man,

grey-haired and lined of face, but still wiry from a life spent mostly in the open air. A kindly man whose servants worshipped him, and who was always ready to pass a cheery word with even the lowliest of his employees, he had the look of one who had known sorrow and tasted of the bitterness of life. The deep-set eyes held a haunted expression, and there was a droop to the sensitive mouth that betrayed a weariness of spirit labouring under the strain of a heavy burden. And in truth Lord Hillingdon carried a burden that was heavy indeed. Few people knew of the secret which had brought Hilary Chase, tenth Earl of Hillingdon, to a premature old age and dulled the brightness of life, for he was a proud man and kept his personal affairs to himself. His wife may have guessed that there was something, but he had never offered her his confidence, and she had never asked for it. He had been a widower when he had married Lucy Salford, eldest daughter of the Earl of Whitsey, and he had never regretted the marriage, for she had proved a sympathetic and understanding wife, whose constant attention had done much to heal the raw wound, the pain of which still lingered even after twenty years.

His second marriage had taken place in the early years of the Great War. There had been no honeymoon; there had been no time for such things in that hectic period. The blow that had brought grey to his hair and despair to his heart had fallen a year later. It fell three months after his son was born, and at forty-five reduced him from a youthful middle age to a man who looked sixty, with all the cares of the world on his shoulders.

His father, the ninth earl, died three years later and Hilary Chase inherited the title, and the estate. During the years that followed he devoted himself to looking after the property. His son grew up, went to Eton, and later to Oxford; and the secret, which was an ever-present source of care and worry, began by slow degrees to grow less formidable. And then his increasing confidence and peace of mind were suddenly shattered. The knowledge that he had believed to be his alone was known to others.

The first intimation came to him in a

letter; a letter that bore neither date nor signature, which suggested a meeting in a small hotel in London with the writer, and a sufficiently veiled threat that ensured the appointment being kept.

He travelled up to Town, and in the smoking-room of that little Bloomsbury Hotel had met for the first time John Dinsley. The interview was brief. Clearly and concisely Dinsley had revealed what he knew, and the result should he make his knowledge public. There had been no attempt on Hillingdon's part to fight the man. He had capitulated from the beginning, agreeing to the other's monstrous terms without argument, and from that day onwards he had lived over a smouldering volcano, conscious that if he deviated one iota from his bargain it would break into eruption, destroying himself and those he loved in its sulphurous fumes.

The money, although it was a considerable sum, worried him very little, for he was a rich man. It was the horrible insecurity that sapped at his vitality and brought that haunted look to his eyes.

He was contemplating his unpleasant

position now as he walked with bowed head across the trim lawn towards the open windows of his study. For the thousandth time he tried to seek some satisfactory way of extricating himself from the quagmire into which, through no fault of his own, he had fallen. Once again, as so many times before, he contemplated the possibility of taking his wife into his confidence, only to reject the idea almost before it had formed in his mind. No, he must continue to bear his burden alone; there was nothing else for it. Only one ray of comfort was vouchsafed to him, and that was that his secret was safe as long as he regularly paid the price that had been demanded. It was a stiff one. Already fifteen thousand pounds had passed into the hands of the three men who had the power to destroy him.

Fifteen thousand pounds represented eighteen months of security. It was a large sum, but not too large for what it had bought. And according to their lights they had dealt fairly. They had kept the arrangement without attempting to increase their demands.

He lifted his head as he heard the sound of a step on the gravel and saw the youthful figure of his secretary coming towards him. Alan Wargreave was excited, as the expression on his face testified.

'Have you heard the news, sir?' he said, as he came within earshot.

Lord Hillingdon frowned slightly and shook his head.

'News? What news, Alan?' he asked.

'There's been two murders,' answered Wargreave, a little breathlessly. 'Those two fellows, Preston Flood and Baldock, have been killed. The whole village is talking about it.'

Lord Hillingdon's breath hissed through his teeth as he drew it in sharply.

'Geoffrey Baldock and Preston Flood?' he repeated. 'Killed?'

Wargreave nodded, a little surprised at the effect of his news.

'Yes. Deuced mysterious business. They were shot with glass arrows. It's like a book — '

'Come into the study,' broke in Lord Hillingdon abruptly, 'and tell me more about it.'

He led the way towards the open windows, his secretary following. How would this affect his own position? His face was anxious as he entered the big, book-lined room and motioned Alan Wargreave to a chair. Would anything be found? The police would, naturally, make a thorough search of both Flood's and Baldock's effects. Had they kept anything that was likely to reflect on him — anything that might reveal the secret, which he had kept for so many years?

'Tell me all you know about it,' he said curtly, and Alan eyed the face of his employer curiously. It was grey and troubled and the thin hands were working nervously. He had never expected that his news would affect the old man like this.

'It seems a most curious business,' he began. 'Flood was killed in the ruins of the old abbey at Claydon, and Baldock at the bottom of his own garden . . . '

Rapidly he repeated what he had heard, and Lord Hillingdon listened with strained attention.

'It's certainly a very queer affair,' he commented when Alan concluded. 'Have

— have the police discovered any clue to the murderer?'

'Not so far as I know,' said his secretary. 'Of course, I only got the information second-hand, and I daresay quite a lot of it is garbled. You know how the people round here exaggerate everything. But I did hear that it was Trevor Lowe, the dramatist, who made the discovery of the first crime, and that he's working in conjunction with Inspector Noyes, of Middlethorpe.'

'Trevor Lowe? I remember being introduced to him once.' Hillingdon pursed his lips. 'How did he come to be mixed up in it?'

'He's staying in the district with a friend of his for a holiday,' said the news-gatherer. 'A man called Medlock, who used to be a reporter in Fleet Street. The fellow was showing him the ruins when they made the discovery. It's going to be a tremendous sensation.'

Hillingdon passed a nervous hand across his lips.

'You say these two men were killed with glass arrows?' he asked suddenly. 'Extraordinary!'

135

'It's amazing,' agreed his secretary. 'That's what's going to appeal so strongly to the public. If they'd been shot with a pistol or poisoned or stabbed I don't suppose it would have been more than a nine days' wonder. But the papers are bound to seize on a murder committed by such bizarre weapons — ' He broke off and gazed anxiously at his employer. 'You look awfully queer, sir,' he said. 'Can I get you something?'

'No, no. I'm all right.' Lord Hillingdon waved the suggestion away impatiently. 'Naturally this has been rather a shock to me.'

'Why?' asked Alan. 'You didn't know either of these men — '

'No, no. I didn't know them,' said Hillingdon. 'But they — well, they were residents, almost neighbours, and therefore — I suppose the fact that they've met violent deaths has given me rather a shock.'

Wargreave was puzzled. He could have understood a natural interest, but he couldn't see why the deaths of two practically complete strangers should affect his employer so keenly. Had he been able to see into the seething state of Lord Hillingdon's mind at that moment he might have understood better.

The news had not only shocked him, it had dazed him. He found it difficult to think coherently. It was not that he felt any grief or concern over the deaths of these two men. What was troubling him was concern for himself and whether the murders would affect his own position adversely. Was there anything to show that he had been in any way connected with these people? Anything that was likely to bring to light the thing he had gone to so much trouble to keep hidden?

'There's one curious thing.' Alan's voice broke in on his thoughts. 'It seems that the person who committed the murders went to Flood's house after killing Flood and cleared out the safe. The police found it open and empty when they got there.'

'Cleared out the safe,' repeated Hillingdon, and he was thinking what that safe might have contained.

Alan nodded.

'Yes. Opened it with Flood's own key,'

he continued. 'Whoever it was, he must have had some nerve, for he had to come to the house in broad daylight, take the risk of being seen by the servants, and make his escape again. It was pretty cool, don't you think?'

'Yes. — Yes, very.' Lord Hillingdon spoke absently.

'Was — was Baldock burgled, too?'

'I haven't heard anything about it,' answered Wargreave shaking his bead. 'Of course, you can't take any of this as absolute fact. As I said before, you know how the people about here exaggerate. There's some talk about Dinsley being suspected. But nobody seems to know why.'

'Dinsley?'

'Yes,' said Alan, and this time he looked troubled. 'I don't suppose there's any truth in it. The rumour seems to have started merely because the police paid him a visit, which is only natural, seeing that he was acquainted with the dead men . . .'

The telephone bell rang, suddenly and unexpectedly. The shrill summons caused them both to start. Wargreave went over to the writing table and picked up the instrument.

'Hello!' he called, and then his voice changed. 'Yes, this is Alan speaking. Yes . . . I've heard. They told me in the post office an hour ago . . . Just a moment and I'll see.' He turned. 'Will you be wanting me this afternoon, sir?' he asked.

Lord Hillingdon started out of a reverie.

'Eh! What's that?' he demanded.

The secretary repeated his question.

''No, no! There's nothing I want you for, if you wish to go out.'

'Thank you,' said Wargreave, and turning again to the instrument. 'Yes, I'll be able to come . . . Four o'clock then.' He put the telephone gently back on its rack and returned to his chair.

'Who was that?' asked his employer.

'Er — a fellow I know at the White Hart,' answered Wargreave untruthfully, and Lord Hillingdon was too occupied to see the slight flush that had come into his secretary's cheeks.

He knew nothing of that young man's

acquaintanceship with Ilene Dinsley, and would have been both perturbed and annoyed had he been aware that it was the girl who had just rung up.

12

The Man Who Scored Golds

The girl was waiting for him that afternoon when he reached the appointed meeting place, and he was shocked to see how pale and worried she looked.

'Why, what's the trouble, Ilene?' he greeted. 'Has your father been troublesome again?'

She shook her head.

'No, it's not that this time,' she answered. 'I'm so glad to see you, Alan. Did it matter, my ringing up?'

'Not as it happened,' he answered. 'I was there to take the message. Otherwise it might have been — well, a little awkward.'

'If you hadn't been there I shouldn't have said who it was,' she replied. 'Why does Lord Hillingdon dislike me?'

He shook his head.

'I don't know,' he said. 'I told you what happened when I mentioned you once.'

The occasion of which he spoke had occurred some months previously, before he had come to know the girl who walked at his side. He had seen her several times, and had once mentioned to his employer that he thought her rather attractive. Lord Hillingdon's comment had astonished him.

'You will have nothing to do with that woman, Wargreave!' he said sternly. 'You understand me? You're to have nothing to do with her while you are in my employ.' And in spite of Alan's questions he had refused to give any explanations concerning his reasons.

Later, when Wargreave had got to know the girl, he had asked her why Lord Hillingdon should adopt this attitude, but she had been unable to offer a suggestion. In consequence, when their acquaintance had ripened into friendship and something more, he had kept the fact from the old man's knowledge. He hated the deception, but Hillingdon's attitude on that first instance had been so uncompromising that he had considered it unnecessary to risk anything in the nature of a 'split' between them.

His position was not entirely the usual one between employer and employee. He was the son of an old friend of Hillingdon's and his father had died when he was a youngster, leaving barely sufficient money to supply the boy with a microscopic income.

Hillingdon, acting as trustee to the small estate, had arranged for his schooling out of his own pocket, and later taken him into his employment. Therefore he was loath to do anything that would upset the older man, whom he regarded affectionately.

'Why did you want to see me so urgently?' he asked, glancing sideways at the girl as they turned off into a narrow lane that led away from the stile, which had been the appointed meeting place.

'I've been worried. Terribly worried,' she answered.

'Why? What's happened?' he asked anxiously. 'You told me it wasn't your father — '

'It is not,' she broke in. 'It's you!'

'Me?' He stopped and stared at her in astonishment. 'Why? What have I done, Ilene?'

143

Her troubled eyes met his, and then dropped.

'I — ' she began, stopped abruptly, and then went on hesitantly: 'Alan, did you know Mr. Flood and Mr. Baldock?'

'Know them?' His surprised expression deepened. 'I've spoken to them, of course, if that's what you mean.'

'It's not quite what I mean,' she said quickly. 'I don't know quite how to put it without making you angry. Did you — were they — ' She became incoherent in her nervousness.

'Now listen.' He took her gently by the shoulders. ''What is the trouble? And what has Flood and Baldock got to do with it?'

'They were murdered,' she whispered in a low voice. 'Killed with glass arrows.' She looked up at him as she spoke and forced herself to meet his gaze steadily.

'Yes, I know that,' he said wonderingly, his brows drawn together in a puzzled frown, 'I heard it at the post office.'

'Well, don't you understand?' she insisted a little impatiently.

He shook his head helplessly.

'I'm afraid I don't, dear,' he replied. 'What are you getting at?'

'I'm getting at this, Alan.' She took her courage in both hands and spoke rapidly, so rapidly that she stumbled over her words. 'Do you remember telling me some months ago, shortly after we met, that you had belonged to an archery club at Oxford, and that during a competition you'd scored ten golds in succession; one of the highest scores that had ever been made?'

A look of dawning comprehension came into his face, his lips twitched, and then he laughed.

'Don't laugh!' she protested. 'I'm serious.'

'You're a silly little goose,' he said. 'Do you mean to tell me that you've been thinking *I* killed these men?'

'No, no! I never thought anything of the sort!' she answered vehemently. 'But I was afraid the — the police might think so.'

'Because I used to be pretty good at archery at Oxford doesn't prove that I killed Flood and Baldock,' he said. 'Why should the police think I did?'

'Because they were both killed by an arrow,' she answered. 'Don't you see! They'll be looking for somebody who's an expert in archery — naturally they will. And when they find out about you they'll begin to imagine all sorts of things . . . '

There was something in what she said, and he pressed his lips.

'They can think what they like,' he said, after a pause, 'but they can't prove anything. It takes more than suspicion to get a conviction. And even if they discover about my prowess at archery, I don't see that it's going to get 'em very far. I had no motive for killing either Flood or Baldock. I didn't like them, but I had no reason to kill them.'

'Could you prove that you didn't?' she asked, her anxiety by no means appeased. 'Where were you, Alan, at the time these men were killed?'

'I don't know.' He frowned. 'I went for a long walk this morning. I rather hoped I might see you, but I didn't.'

'Alone?' she said.

'Yes, of course,' he replied.

'There you are!' she broke in quickly. 'You couldn't prove that you didn't kill these men.'

He slipped an arm tenderly round her shoulders.

'Don't be silly, Ilene,' he said soothingly. 'Your nerves are all upset. I'm not surprised, considering the life you've had lately, darling. You're just worrying yourself about nothing. I assure you there's not a particle of evidence to connect me with these crimes.'

She hid her face on his shoulder and he smoothed her hair.

'I've been worrying ever since they told me how these men had been murdered,' she said in a muffled voice.

'Ever since who told you?' he asked.

'The police. Didn't you know? They came to interview father this morning,' she replied. 'I've been scared to death ever since.'

'Well, there's no need to be scared any longer,' he said. 'I give you my word, Ilene, that I know nothing about these murders. Though I must say it was an extraordinary weapon to choose.'

'That's just it!' she said, her fears returning. 'Whoever used it must have been an expert. They'll find out about that competition, Alan — '

'Nonsense!' he interrupted almost irritably. 'And even if they do it doesn't matter. There are lots of people in the world who are good at archery.'

'But not in West Dorling,' she said meaningfully. 'They'll find out and they'll come and question you, and — '

'Well, that won't worry me. They can come and question me as much as they like,' he answered lightly.

'You're not cross, are you?' she asked apprehensively, and for an answer he kissed her.

'Of course I'm not,' he said. 'It was rather dear of you. But now forget all about it. Let's walk through to Middlethorpe and have tea at the Old Forge, shall we?'

She acquiesced, and they both set off down the lane side by side; and Mr. Gormley, who had both seen and heard the interview, waited until they had passed out of sight before emerging from his place of concealment behind the tall hedge.

★ ★ ★

Doctor Chambers came down the path of the little cottage garden, opened the gate, and passed out into the High Street. As he turned in the direction of the Green, the gaunt man who had been coming towards him on the opposite side crossed over.

'Good afternoon, Doctor,' greeted John Dinsley. 'Been visiting poor Ollen?'

Chambers nodded shortly. He disliked the man and was not best pleased at being accosted.

'Yes,' he said. 'He's still unconscious, but I've every hope that he'll recover. The person or persons responsible ought to be publicly horsewhipped.'

'Don't you think it's just possible they were not to blame?' suggested Dinsley. 'It's very dark at the bend. Perhaps they were unaware that they'd hit anything.'

'They couldn't have been unaware,' said Chambers. 'They must have known.

149

The man was flung onto the pavement, and anyway their lights would have revealed him. It was just sheer callousness!'

'You feel very strongly about it,' said Dinsley, with a sour smile.

'I do!' declared Chambers. 'Very strongly indeed. Poor Ollen was a hardworking, decent man, and now, even if he recovers, he'll be incapacitated for life. It's enough to make anyone feel strongly.' He glanced ostentatiously at his watch. 'I'm afraid I must be going,' he said quickly. 'I have another patient to see.' This was untrue, for he had been merely on his way to tea.

'I won't detain you,' said the other, and with a nod he moved on down the street.

The man who had halted to gaze into the window of a little general shop higher up also moved on, and Doctor Chambers, noting the fact, drew his own conclusions. So Dinsley was under observation, was he? Well, he supposed that was only natural. The cigarette end that had been discovered in the ruins of the abbey was sufficient to bring him under suspicion.

Reaching his cottage, he let himself in and ordered tea from the woman who came daily to attend to his needs. There were several letters and messages, among them a notification from the police that the inquest would be held at ten o'clock in the forenoon on the day after tomorrow.

His mind went back to the conversation with Sergeant Akeman and the prophecy he had made which had been so amply fulfilled.

While he ate his tea he allowed his thoughts to dwell on the circumstances surrounding the two murders, and then, dismissing the matter, went into his small dispensary to make up certain medicines which he had prescribed.

By the time he had finished this task and neatly wrapped the bottles and boxes up ready for dispatch the first of his evening patients had arrived, and he was kept busy until well past nine.

His frugal supper was waiting for him when he had dealt with his last case and he was ready for it. After a cigarette and a glance at the paper, and thoroughly tired, he went to bed. It seemed to him that his head had barely touched the pillow before the shrill clang of the night bell woke him with a start. But he must have been asleep several hours, for as he sat up and switched on the light the clock on his bedside table showed him it was half-past two.

The bell pealed again, and he got wearily out of bed, thrust his feet into a pair of slippers, drew on a dressing gown, and hurried down the stairs. Opening the front door, he peered into the darkness.

'What is it?' he demanded sleepily, as he saw the shadowy figure standing on the step.

'Will you come along at once to Mrs. Ollen, sir?' said an agitated voice. 'Joe Ollen's dead! 'E's been stabbed!'

13

The Night Slayer

The oil lamp threw a dim light over the small, low-ceilinged room, leaving most of it in shadow, but flooding the narrow truckle bed by the window so that the sprawling figure which lay there was revealed clearly to the three men who stood grouped nearby.

Inspector Noyes, rather sketchily attired owing to the hastiness with which he had obeyed the summons, emitted a subdued barrage of guttural noises and rubbed thoughtfully at his unshaven chin.

'Queer business,' he muttered, without removing his eyes from the body of the dead man. 'What motive could anyone have for wanting to kill a feller like Joe Ollen?'

Doctor Chambers shook his head.

'Ask me another,' he replied in a low voice. 'But somebody must have had a good reason.'

Inspector Noyes pursed his lips.

'It wasn't difficult,' he said, jerking his head towards the open window at the top part of a ladder, which was visible above the sill. 'The killer never had to enter the room at all. He only had to climb the ladder and lean through the window. And he only had an unconscious man to deal with. It was easy. Who made the discovery?'

'Mrs. Ollen,' said the doctor. 'I had suggested that she should keep an eye on her husband in case he recovered consciousness. So she arranged to visit him every two hours. She made the discovery at two o'clock, roused the man next door, and sent him round to inform me.'

'Where is Mrs. Ollen?' The Inspector turned to the shadowy constable who was hovering in the background.

'I'm here, sir,' said a husky voice, and a stout, grey-haired, tearful woman came timidly forward.

'Tell me, Mrs. Ollen,' said Noyes gently, his usual bellow subdued to a sympathetic undertone. 'You heard nothing before you came in and found your husband — like this?' He half-turned back towards the blood-stained bed.

'No, sir,' answered the woman with a catch in her voice. 'I 'eard nothin' at all! After I'd been to 'ave a look at Joe at twelve I lay down for a bit, and I must 'ave dropped asleep. I'd set the alarm for two, and it woke me. I came in to see if 'e was all right and found 'im lyin' just as 'e is now, 'alf out of the bed and covered in blood.' Her voice broke and she began to sob violently.

The Inspector laid his hand on her plump shoulder.

'There, there, Mrs. Ollen, brace up,' he said soothingly. 'It must have given you a pretty bad shock.' He turned to the constable. 'Take her downstairs and make her some tea.'

The red-faced policeman took the weeping woman gently by the arm and led her away. Noyes came back to the doctor's side.

'During that two hours, while she was asleep,' he said thoughtfully, 'Ollen was killed.'

'That would coincide with my opinion of the time at which death took place,' agreed Chambers.

'He must have been a cool customer,' muttered the Inspector, 'whoever did it. Where did he get the ladder from?'

'It was kept on the premises,' said the doctor. 'Ollen used to do odd painting jobs in his spare time. He kept the ladder near a little tool shed at the bottom of the garden.'

'Everything to hand,' muttered Noyes. 'He took the knife away with him, unfortunately.'

In the silence that followed, the rasping of his fingers on his bristly chin could be heard distinctly.

'It's a mysterious business,' he went on, after a pause, 'and I can't see any sense in it. Why kill a man like Ollen? Nobody had anything to gain. West Dorling 'ull be getting a bad reputation if this goes on. Two men killed by glass arrows and one man stabbed, all within forty-eight hours.'

'I suppose,' suggested Chambers, 'there's no connection?'

'How could there be?' Noyes swung round towards him.

'I don't know,' answered the doctor, shrugging his shoulders. 'It only crossed my mind.'

'Baldock and Flood were killed by arrows,' said Noyes, shaking his head. 'And this man was stabbed with a knife. Besides, there's nothing to link 'em up, so far as I can see.'

'Or so far as I can see,' confessed Chambers. 'I was only offering a suggestion.'

'I'll bear it in mind, of course,' said the Inspector, 'but I don't think anything's likely to come of it. Let's go and have a look outside. There's nothing more to be learned here.'

He left the bedroom, closing and locking the door behind him, and accompanied by Chambers made his way down the narrow staircase and out into the little front garden.

The room which had been assigned to Joe Ollen after his accident faced the back, and a narrow passageway between the cottage and the wooden fence dividing it from the next house led round to the rear. The Inspector made his way to the back of the premises and paused beneath the ladder, which was reared up against the open window of the dead man's room. Taking a torch from his pocket, he directed its light on the ground in the vicinity of the ladder and made a careful search. But there were no useful traces to be found. The path had been made up with cinders, and although these were disturbed and there were obvious marks they were none of them clear enough to afford a tangible clue.

After some time Noyes straightened up and pocketed his torch.

'Nothing here at all,' he grunted disappointedly. 'The man must have known something about the place, though, for he evidently came expecting to find the ladder. The knowledge that there was a ladder must have given him the idea.'

'Half the village knew,' said Chambers. 'I don't think that's going to lead you anywhere.'

'I don't suppose it will, sir,' grunted the Inspector gloomily. 'But it's a fact, and that's all I can do at the moment, collect facts.'

He sighed and yawned, for he was a very tired man. His exertions during the day had sent him to bed weary, and his sudden awakening had left him unrested and sleepy.

'I had quite enough to contend with without this,' he grumbled. 'This 'ull mean another inquest.'

They went back to the cottage, and met the constable just coming out to find them.

'How's Mrs. Ollen now?' asked Noyes.

'She be a bit better, sir,' answered the stolid policeman. 'The cup o' tea seemed to do 'er good. I was just comin' to see whether you and the doctor 'ud like one.'

'I should!' said Noyes, and Chambers added his affirmative.

The man retired, and presently re-appeared with two large steaming cups. They both drank the scalding tea gratefully, and felt better.

'Well, I'll be getting along, I think,' said Chambers, setting down the empty cup. 'You don't want me any more at the moment, do you, Inspector?'

Noyes shook his head.

'No, sir,' he answered. 'There's nothing more you can do and very little that I can do for the matter of that. So far as

I can see, the only thing to be done is to set the usual routine inquiries going finding out whether Ollen had any enemies, and check up where they were at the time the murder was committed.'

His tone implied that he didn't expect to gain anything very much from these proceedings, and leaving him Doctor Chambers set off towards the Green to resume his interrupted sleep.

When he was alone Noyes walked out into the darkness of the garden and took a puff or two at a surreptitious pipe. By the time he got back Mrs. Ollen was sufficiently calm to be questioned, which he did as gently and sympathetically as possible. But he learned nothing. So far as she could inform him her husband had had no enemies and she was completely unable to suggest any reason for his murder.

Noyes, a tired and baffled man, went back to the station house no wiser than when he had stood staring down at Ollen's body. The crime was meaningless — a wanton killing that had neither rhyme nor reason.

14

Information from the Yard

The entire village was humming with the murder of Joe Ollen on the following morning. Coming, as it had, immediately on the top of the other two crimes, it created a sensation the like of which West Dorling had never experienced.

The milkman brought the news to Mrs. Jiffer, and that excited and voluble woman related it with ghoulish pleasure to Trevor Lowe and Tom Medlock when she brought up their morning tea.

The dramatist was only mildly interested. His mind was too fully occupied with the glass arrow murders for him to spare more than passing attention to the fate that had overtaken the unfortunate Joe Ollen. For it was not until some time afterwards that he began to wonder whether there was any connection.

'Heard the latest, Lowe?' Medlock, a

tousle-headed, sleepy-eyed apparition, clutching a dressing gown round him, appeared just as Mrs. Jiffer had finished her highly-coloured narrative.

'Mrs. Jiffer has just been telling me,' nodded his friend.

'What do you think of it?' grunted the reporter, perching himself on the edge of the bed and running his fingers through his hair. 'By Jove, it never rains but it pours! Three murders, one on top of the other. Old Bishop 'ull go raving mad with excitement.'

Lowe set down his empty cup on the bedside table.

'D'you know anything about Ollen?' he inquired.

Medlock shook his head.

'Only that he was a very respectable, hard-working fellow,' he answered. 'Why anyone should want to kill him I can't imagine.'

'No, it's queer,' agreed the dramatist thoughtfully. 'However, our main concern at the moment is with the other business, and I don't see how this murder can come into it.'

'I don't either,' said the reporter. 'Still, it's a funny thing, and I'm going to follow it up. I'll help to keep the public's interest alive until we've got something more about the glass arrow killings.'

Lowe made a grimace.

'You're a conscienceless beggar!' he remarked. 'I believe you'd be willing for the whole population to die in order to provide you with copy for your infernal newspaper.'

Medlock grinned.

'Not quite as bad as that,' he protested. 'Still I must say I like to be in a position to supply the goods. What are you proposing to do today?'

Lowe was evasive. He had, as a matter of fact, no settled plan. He had already carried out his project and written to the secretary of the Toxophilite Society asking for a list of its members for the last thirty years, and until he received a reply he was content to more or less mark time. The suggestions he had put up to Inspector Noyes were, he knew, being carried out by that conscientious official.

In the meanwhile there was very little

he could do. Medlock went off to have his bath, and while he waited for his host to vacate the bathroom Lowe mulled over all the facts in his possession. They were not many, and he was a little dismayed at how meager was his knowledge.

Here were three men who had come to reside in the district within a few months of each other. They were, on the surface at any rate, not very friendly. They all appeared to have money and had lived in a style commensurate with large incomes. Where had this money come from? According to what Doctor Chambers had heard while passing through the wood on his way home the source was illegal, or at any rate there was something concerning them which was not open and above-board. Of these three men two had met violent deaths — deaths that had been brought about by a most unusual weapon, an arrow of glass. They had both been killed on the same morning and obviously by the same hand. The question was why, and what significance was attached to the method of the killing?

Lowe lay back on his pillow and stared

at the yellow sunlight beyond the lattice window. It seemed only reasonable to suppose that the motive concerned them all, since there was obviously a connecting link between them and since the weapon used in each case was the same. But what was this connecting link? If the unknown killer was out to murder the three surely Dinsley would have shown some knowledge of the reason. Yet Lowe was prepared to swear that that surly and unprepossessing man was as much in the dark as he was himself. He was afraid, yes, but he was afraid merely because his two associates had been killed and he naturally wondered whether his turn was coming. But he was unaware of the reason they had been killed or who was responsible.

The glass arrow conveyed nothing to him. Yet the murderer must have decided on the weapon because of some special significance it possessed. Nobody in their right senses would have used such an unusual method unless there was a very good reason for doing so. It would have been far easier to have shot Flood and

Baldock than to have killed them in the way that had been chosen.

But if Dinsley saw nothing in the use of the arrow his daughter had certainly done so. The weapon had been the reason for that look of fear that had come to her eyes. She either knew or suspected what lay behind the arrow, and was terrified in consequence.

After breakfast Medlock announced his intention of going over to Noyes.

'I want to get particulars of this Ollen business,' he said.

'I'll come with you,' remarked Lowe, and they set off together.

They found Inspector Noyes in his little office, tired and harassed.

'I don't know that I can give you any information for publication, Mr. Medlock,' he said, shaking his head. 'Ollen was killed by some person unknown between twelve and two o'clock this morning. That's all I can tell you.'

'That's all right to start with,' said the reporter cheerfully. 'Who made the discovery and how was he killed?'

'The discovery was made by his wife,

and he was stabbed with a knife that was taken away by the murderer,' said Noyes reluctantly. 'And that's all I can tell you, Mr. Medlock.'

Medlock shrugged his shoulders resignedly.

'Oh, well,' he said. 'I shall have to make do with that, and any other information I can pick up in the village. So long, Lowe. I'll see you later.'

He took his departure and Noyes lay back in his chair with a yawn.

'Excuse me, sir,' he apologised, 'but I'm dead beat. I had very little sleep last night.'

'I don't suppose you did,' said Lowe sympathetically. Have you any idea why this man Ollen was killed?'

The Inspector shook his head.

'Not the faintest,' he declared candidly. 'It's as big a mystery as the other affair. Why anyone should want to go to the trouble and risk of murdering a man like Ollen is beyond me.'

'Tell me more about it,' said the dramatist, and Noyes complied. When he had finished Lowe pursed his lips.

'Extraordinary!' he murmured. 'It looks as if there were two killers at large in West Dorling.'

'And equally mysterious,' grunted Noyes, with a volley of hisses.

'Unless,' mused the dramatist, 'this Ollen business is connected with the other.'

'Chambers suggested that,' said the Inspector. 'But I can't see how it can be. Ollen had nothing to do with Flood and Baldock, and they were killed with glass arrows and he was knifed.'

'But why?' murmured Lowe. Now he had heard the details he was beginning to get more interested. 'People don't commit murder without a reason.'

'Do you think this is mixed up with the other affair, then?' asked Noyes.

Lowe shook his head.

'I shouldn't like to go as far as that,' he declared, 'but it's peculiar, and therefore worth considering. Here are two men killed under mysterious circumstances and almost immediately after, another murder takes place under equally mysterious circumstances. The fact that there might be a connection is worth bearing in mind.'

The Inspector sighed.

'It's all rather a hopeless tangle,' he said despondently. 'Perhaps when I get a reply from the Yard it may help.'

'You sent up the dead man's finger-prints?' inquired the dramatist.

'Yes,' answered Noyes. 'I sent 'em yesterday and asked for a reply by return. I also sent one of the arrows, asking if they could trace up where it came from.'

'Well, you can't do more,' said Lowe. 'The solution to the arrow murders, I'm convinced, lies in the past of these three men, Dinsley, Flood and Baldock, and there I think this fellow Gormley may be able to help you.'

'Gormley?' Noyes raised his eyebrows. 'How?'

'Well, he apparently knows something,' explained Lowe, 'about Dinsley, at any rate. What Chambers overheard proves that. And I think it would be worthwhile questioning him.'

'Now why didn't I think of that?' said the Inspector. 'It's a damn good idea, Mr. Lowe, and I'll have it done right away.'

He touched a bell on his desk, and to

the constable who appeared gave an order.

'I'd like to be present when you question him,' said Lowe, when the constable had departed.

'I don't see why not,' said the Inspector. 'Yes, I'll let you know, sir, when they bring him in.'

'In the meanwhile,' the dramatist went on, 'I suppose you're having Dinsley watched?'

'You bet your life I am!' declared Noyes emphatically. 'It's my opinion that he knows more about this business than anyone else — and that daughter of his, too.'

'She knows more than he does, or at least she suspects,' said Lowe.

He broke off as the door opened and a big-built, red-faced man came striding into the little office.

''Morning, Noyes,' greeted the newcomer, in a throaty voice. 'I got your report and I've come along.'

Noyes had risen to his feet and was standing stiffly to attention, and Lowe guessed that this was the Chief Constable.

'Good morning, sir,' said the Inspector.

'I was coming over to see you — '

'Thought I'd save you the trouble,' grunted the red-faced man, taking up a position in front of the microscopic fire-place and looking from one to the other as though he were reviewing a squad of raw recruits. 'Who is — er — who is this gentleman?'

'This gentleman, sir,' answered Noyes, 'is Mr. Trevor Lowe.'

The bushy grey eyebrows rose.

'Mr. Trevor Lowe, huh?' The bushy eyebrows, having reached the highest point of elevation, reversed the procedure and drew down over the prominent eyes. 'How d'you do, sir?'

'This is Major Harland, the Chief Constable.' The Inspector introduced the newcomer, and Lowe inclined his head.

'You were the first person to discover the body of Flood, I believe,' said Major Harland, and when Lowe nodded: 'Extraordinary business! What do you make of it, sir?'

'Up to the present I don't make anything of it,' declared the dramatist candidly. 'Inspector Noyes very kindly

171

allowed me to assist with the investigations, but I'm afraid I haven't been of much use.'

'We're very glad of your assistance all the same,' said the Chief Constable. 'I'm not one of these fellows who believe in doing everything off his own bat. In fact I came here this morning to discuss with Inspector Noyes the advisability of asking for the cooperation of Scotland Yard.'

'I shall be only too pleased, sir,' said Noyes. 'I don't mind admitting that this case is too big for me to handle on my own.'

'Quite! Quite!' said the Major, nodding in agreement. 'And it's not a question of capability, Inspector. You're capable enough. A most capable officer. It's experience. We haven't had much experience with murder cases, eh?'

'No, sir,' said Noyes.

'You agree with me, Mr. Lowe?' The Chief Constable turned a pair of shrewd eyes towards the dramatist.

'Most certainly I do,' he answered. 'This is undoubtedly a case for the wider organization of the Yard.'

'I think so,' said Major Harland. 'I'll get in touch with them this afternoon, and ask 'em to send someone down. At the same time,' he added, 'I hope you'll still continue to give us any assistance you can, Mr. Lowe. I shall be only too pleased to listen to any opinions or suggestions you have to make.'

'Any assistance I can offer is at your disposal,' said the dramatist. 'I must admit, Major, that I am intensely interested. The use of the glass arrow is so unusual that it appeals to my imagination.'

'Absolutely extraordinary!' said the Chief Constable, shaking his head. 'Quite a unique case, I think. Have you ever heard of such a thing before?'

'No,' said Lowe, 'I never have. There have been, I believe, two arrow murders, but an arrow of glass is quite original in my experience.'

'And now, on the top of the other two murders, there's the killing of this poor fellow, Ollen,' grunted the Chief Constable. 'Another mysterious business. Have you got any further with that?'

173

Noyes, to whom the question had been addressed, shook his head.

'No, I'm afraid not, sir, at present,' he said.

'It looks as though an epidemic of murder has broken out in the district,' said the Major, frowning. 'What type of investigation are you following?'

Noyes explained briefly, and the Chief Constable listened without comment.

'It seems to me,' he remarked, when the Inspector had finished, 'that we're doing everything possible. Perhaps the report on these fingerprints will throw some light on the matter. Do you think the solution is to be found in the pasts of these men?'

'I think it's probable,' said Lowe. 'After all, you can't have an effect without a cause. The effect, in this instance, is two dead men, and the cause is the reason why they were killed.'

The telephone bell rang as he finished speaking, and with an apology Noyes picked up the instrument.

'Hello!' he called. "Yes, this is Middlethorpe police station. Inspector Noyes speaking. Oh yes . . . ' He looked round. 'It's from the Yard,' he said. 'Yes . . . no, no trace at all. Thank you very much. Goodbye.' His expression was disappointed as he hung up the receiver. 'That was from the fingerprints department,' he explained. 'They have no record of either Baldock or Flood's fingerprints. Confirmation in writing, follows.'

'Which means,' grunted the Chief Constable, 'that they weren't crooks after all.'

'We can hardly be as definite as that, Major,' said Lowe. 'It only shows that they were never convicted.'

'Yes. Yes, I suppose so,' agreed the Chief Constable. 'All the same, it doesn't help us much, does it?'

'No, I'm afraid it doesn't,' said the dramatist, frowning. 'We shall have to — '

He was interrupted by a tap on the door and the appearance of the desk sergeant.

'What is it, Beecher?' asked Noyes impatiently.

'The constable's got that feller outside, sir,' answered the sergeant. 'Do you want to see him now?'

'Fellow, what fellow?' grunted Noyes, and then, as he remembered: 'Oh, you mean Gormley.'

'Yes, sir.' Beecher waited expectantly.

'That's quick work,' said the Inspector. 'I wonder how they got hold of him so soon. All right, Beecher, bring him in.'

15

The Questioning of Mr. Gormley

The reason for what Inspector Noyes had so correctly described as 'quick work' was due to a remarkable piece of luck on the part of the constable who had been detailed to bring Mr. Gormiey to the station house.

This man had once been loaned to West Dorling to replace a fellow policeman who had been laid low with influenza, and the little, wizened man was known to him by sight.

Setting out on his errand he had seen a familiar figure shuffling along Middlethorpe's narrow High Street, and he stopped the police car with a benediction on the kind fate which had intervened to save him a journey.

Mr. Gormley, having completed the business which had brought him to the neighbouring town, was contemplating returning to his cottage when he heard himself addressed by name, and turned in surprise. His surprise changed to apprehension when he saw the car and the uniformed man it contained.

'Excuse me.' The policeman was polite. 'Excuse me, but I was just on the way to see you.'

'To see me?' Mr. Gormley's whining voice held a note of fear. 'What d'you want to see me for?'

'Inspector Noyes would like to have a word with you,' said the policeman, and a little reluctantly he added: 'sir.'

''Ave a word with me? What about?' demanded Mr. Gormley. 'I've done nothin' wrong. What does 'e want with me?'

'I can't tell you that,' answered the constable. 'I'm merely following my instructions, and they was to take you to Inspector Noyes. Will you step into the car?'

Mr. Gormley complied with reluctance, his mind by no means at peace. This was an unexpected incident, and it filled him with uneasiness. What did the police want him for? What had they discovered? It couldn't be anything very serious or the man at his side would have been less polite. This offered a modicum of comfort. He knew from experience that this was a more or less friendly interview that awaited him. Had it not been, the invitation would have been couched more peremptorily.

The police car came to a halt outside the station house, and getting down the constable waited for Mr. Gormley to alight.

'Come this way, please,' he said, and the shabby little man followed him up the steps and into the charge room.

The desk sergeant eyed him curiously, and he affected a nonchalance he was far from feeling.

'Will you tell the Inspector that I've brought the man he wanted to see?' said the constable. 'The name's Gormley.'

The grey-haired man behind the high desk nodded, gave Mr. Gormley another curious glance, and, getting heavily down from his stool, crossed over to a door on which he tapped. Disappearing into the room beyond he closed the door, and Mr. Gormley heard a rumble of voices. After a short interval the desk sergeant reappeared.

'This way,' he said, and Mr. Gormley shuffled towards him.

He was ushered into a small office containing three men, who stared at him as he stood hesitantly inside the doorway. Inspector Noyes, whom he knew by sight, was sitting behind a littered desk.

'Come in, Mr. Gormley,' he said. 'Sit down, will you.'

He indicated a chair that was drawn up facing him, and Gormley went over to it and perched himself on the edge.

'What's all this about?' he demanded a little truculently. 'What's the idea of making me come here?'

'I think you may be in a position to assist us,' said Noyes. 'I'm inquiring into the deaths of Mr. Flood and Mr. Baldock, and I should like you to answer one or two questions.'

Lowe, who was watching interestedly, saw the thin, wizened face go a shade paler.

'What should I know about it?' demanded Gormley. 'I didn't know either of them. It's no good askin' me anythin'. I can't help you.'

'Well, we shall see,' said the Inspector. 'If you can't there's no harm done. You say you didn't know either Mr. Flood or Mr. Baldock?'

'That's right,' said Gormley. 'I didn't know either of 'em.'

'But you know Mr. Dinsley!' snapped Noyes abruptly.

'Well, I know 'im by sight,' answered Gormley, after a momentary hesitation.

'Only by sight?' persisted the Inspector.

'Well,' — the little man corrected himself hastily — 'I know him to pass the time of day to, that's all.'

'I see.' Noyes had drawn a notepad towards him and was scribbling down his replies. 'You only know him well enough to say how d'you do. Is that it?'

'That's it,' declared Mr. Gormley, shifting uneasily in his chair.

'On the night before the murder of Flood and Baldock did you meet Mr. Dinsley near the footpath in Longman's Spinney?'

Mr. Gormley thought rapidly before he replied. Three pairs of eyes were fixed on him intently, and he realized that unless he was careful it would be quite easy to make a slip.

'I'm not sure that I remember — ' he began in order to gain time.

'Well, will you try and think,' said the Inspector curtly. 'It's most important.'

'I believe,' said Mr. Gormley, 'now you come to mention it, that I did see Mr. Dinsley that night. I was coming through the Spinney and met him, and we remarked on the weather. It was shocking.'

'You held no other conversation with him except to remark on the weather?' inquired Noyes.

'That's all, so far as I can remember.' Mr. Gormley's small eyes were wary. How much did this florid-faced man before him know?

'What happened after that?' said Noyes.

'I walked part of the way with him through the village,' answered Gormley sullenly. 'What's all this leadin' to?'

'It may lead to a lot, it may lead to nothing,' said the Inspector. 'You walked a short way with him through the village. You didn't go into his house?'

'Well, yes, I did, now you bring it to me mind,' said Mr. Gormley. 'It was rainin' like the devil and Mr. Dinsley very kindly suggested I might like somethin' to keep the cold out.'

'I see.' The Inspector's eyes were fixed on his with an unwavering stare. 'You only know him well enough to say how d'you do, and yet he asks you into his house for a drink?'

'Well, it was a wet night,' explained Mr. Gormley. 'I was pretty well soaked, so was 'e. I don't see what all this has got to do with the murder of Flood and Baldock.'

'I'm coming to that,' said Noyes. 'You don't know anything about Dinsley that he wouldn't like made public?'

'Me?' Mr. Gormley infused a note of righteous indignation into his voice. 'What should I know about Mr. Dinsley?'

'I'm asking you,' said the Inspector. 'When you passed this remark to him about the weather, as you say, in Longman's Spinney, why did he reply, 'Yon slimy little rat! Blackmail, eh? Who put you up to this, Haldock'?' He dropped his eyes to consult a slip of paper in front of him as he spoke, and the watchful Lowe saw Gormley catch his breath.

'I don't know what you're talkin' about,' he answered, recovering himself. 'Mr. Dinsley never said anything of the sort. Why should he?'

'That's what I want to know!' retorted Noyes sternly. 'According to my information those were the words he used. And then he said: 'Well, we can't talk here. Come up to the house.'

'I don't know where you got your information from,' declared Gormley, shaking his head emphatically, 'but you've got it all wrong. Mr. Dinsley wouldn't speak like that to me. What you're accusin' me of is tryin' to blackmail him. Is that it?'

'I'm not accusing you of anything,' said the Inspector. 'I'm just asking questions and waiting for you to answer them.'

'Well, I have answered 'em.' The little man stared at him defiantly. 'Mr. Dinsley never used those words, and if anybody said he did he's a liar!'

'Supposing,' Trevor Lowe spoke for the first time. 'Supposing we can bring forward a witness who is prepared to swear he heard Dinsley utter those words, what then?'

Mr. Gormley licked his lips.

'I'd say the same as I've said to the Inspector,' he answered. 'Mr. Dinsley may have used those words to somebody, but it was not me!'

'Are you prepared to swear,' went on the dramatist, 'that you know nothing concerning Mr. Dinsley which would warrant his making such a remark to you?'

'Yes, I'll take me oath on it!' declared Gormley. 'I don't know nothin' at all about Dinsley, much less anythin' he'd be scared of becoming public.'

'What do you do for a living?' asked Lowe suddenly.

'Me?' Mr. Gormley was obviously disconcerted. 'I pick up a bit here and there, and I've got a little private money of my own.'

'You've never been in a permanent job?' persisted the dramatist.

'Well, yes I have.' Gormley was growing more and more uncomfortable at the barrage of questions. 'I used to be in a solicitor's office in my younger days. But I don't see what it's got to do with you. You've no right to go asking me all these questions. I've nothing to do with these murders, and you can't prove that I have.'

'According to the law,' said Lowe quietly, 'which you should know very well, Gormley, any member of the public can be questioned so long as they are not asked anything which is likely to convict them.'

'That's right,' said Mr. Gormley. 'But that's what you're tryin' to do. You're tryin' to make me say that I was usin' knowledge concernin' Mr. Dinsley to force him to pay me to keep quiet.' He looked from one to the other triumphantly. 'Isn't that askin' me to convict meself? If you want to question anybody why don't you question Mr. Dinsley? Ask him if I've ever tried to blackmail him. He'll soon tell you the truth.'

'I wonder if he would,' murmured the dramatist.

'Well, if he won't that's his business, ain't it?' said the little man. 'But you're not goin' to mix me up in somethin' I don't know nothin' about, and that's flat!'

They were at a disadvantage, and they knew it, and to judge by his rapidly returning self-confidence, so did Mr. Gormley.

'We're not trying to mix you up in anything,' grunted the Chief Constable, who had listened up to now in silence. 'We're merely trying to gather information. And since information reached us that you were in a position to supply us with certain facts we naturally decided to question you.'

'Well, and now I've told you I know nothin', what then?' demanded Mr. Gormley.

'Then,' said Lowe smoothly, before either the Chief Constable or Inspector Noyes could reply, 'we can only apologize for wasting your time and causing you any small amount of inconvenience.'

'I should think so, too!' snarled Gormley, secure in the knowledge that he had defeated them. 'Detainin' a respectable citizen and treatin' 'im as if 'e was a criminal. If I liked to make a fuss about this you'd be in a nasty position — all the lot of you!'

'Now, it's no good taking that line — '
began Major Harland.

'If Mr. Gormley wishes to take any
action,' said Lowe smoothly, 'I should
advise him to do so. His wiser course,
however, which I am sure he will realize
when he has time to think the matter
over, will be to say no more about it.'

The softness of his voice and the
mildness of his manner gave Gormley a
false sense of his advantage.

'I don't know that I'm prepared — ' he
began.

'Otherwise,' said the dramatist, inter-
rupting him, 'it may be necessary to
inquire into the circumstances which
made Mr. Gormley give up a permanent
position in a solicitor's office and live by
— making a bit here and there.'

Mr. Gormley gulped. The bluster faded
as swiftly as an unfixed photographic
print in the rays of a noonday sun.

'Well, if you don't want me any more
I'll be going,' he muttered, and rising to
his feet shuffled towards the door.

Nobody made any attempt to stop him,
and after hesitating a second he twisted

the handle, jerked open the door, and disappeared into the charge room. There was a moment's silence after he'd gone, and then the Chief Constable expelled his pent-up breath.

'That took the wind out of his sails,' he grunted. 'A nasty piece of work, eh?'

'Very nasty,' agreed Lowe. 'I don't think there's any doubt that he does know something about Dinsley and *did* try to blackmail the man.'

'Neither do I, sir,' said Noyes. 'Although the trouble is, I doubt if Chambers could swear that Dinsley was speaking to him. He didn't overhear what Gormley said. He only recognized him by the tone of his voice, and I doubt if that would be sufficient for us to take any further action!'

'He knows something about Dinsley,' murmured the dramatist. 'And he knows something about Flood and Baldock, too. In fact I'm pretty sure he knows just what those three were doing in West Doring, and where the money came from which enabled them to live in the style they did.'

'But does he know anything about the murders?' grunted Major Harland.

'He's not responsible for them!' declared Lowe with conviction. 'That type of man hasn't got the nerve to commit murder, apart from the fact that I should very much doubt if he's ever handled a bow and arrow in his life.'

'But he may know who did,' said the Chief Constable.

And in this he was nearer the truth than he guessed, for Mr. Stephen Gormley had, that night, arranged to meet the man whose hand had released the bow string which had sent those glittering arrows of glass into the hearts of Preston Flood and Geoffrey Baldock, and exact payment for his silence.

16

I, Said the Fly

Mr. Gormely returned home a little shaken by his unpleasant experience. His buxom landlady brought him his tea, and over it he reviewed the situation.

The fact that his meeting with Dinsley in the Spinney had been overheard by someone had given him a shock, but taking it all round he thought he had emerged from the interview fairly satisfactorily. It was that last remark of Lowe's that had given him cause for uneasiness. There was a great deal in Mr. Gormley's life that he preferred should remain hidden.

He came to the conclusion that he had been a little foolish in adopting the high-handed attitude that he had attempted. It had been bad policy. It had antagonized the police without achieving any other result than to offer a sop to his wounded vanity.

Yes, decidedly he had been wrong. However, very little harm had been done, and under the stimulating influence of his tea he allowed his mind to drift into more pleasant channels.

His immediate plans were complete. Dinsley he was sure of. On the following afternoon he had arranged to meet that mean and unpleasant man and put forward his final ultimatum. There would be trouble. Dinsley would bluff and bluster. He was prepared for that. But eventually he would capitulate. He couldn't do anything else, because he held the whip hand. Dinsley would have to do as he was told or — well, the result would be most unpleasant for him.

And that other man, the man who had killed Flood and Baldock. He would have to do as he was told, too. For whereas Dinsley, if he kicked, would get seven years, that other would go to the trap. There was no doubt of that. His evidence, if he liked to open his mouth, would send him there.

Mr. Gormley smiled sourly as he finished his third cup of tea and lit a cigarette. Yes, he couldn't get out of it. It would be no good attempting violence. He had taken certain precautions, and he had been careful to mention these in the telephone message he had put through that morning.

There was a barn midway between West Dorling and Middlethorpe, which he had chosen as the meeting place. At twelve at night it was unlikely there would be anyone abroad to witness the meeting. The matter would not take very long. It was merely a question of arranging terms. That was one of the things that occasioned him a considerable amount of thought. It was no good asking too much, but at the same time it would be ridiculous to ask too little. His silence was worth a lot. He was offering a life in exchange, and a life was valuable — at least to the person concerned.

But it was no good asking for something that was beyond the other's power to give, and this was what bothered him. For he was unaware exactly how much the man was worth.

He turned the matter over in his mind for an hour or more, coming eventually to the conclusion that it was a matter for discussion.

He had his supper at nine o'clock, and deciding that it would take him a little over half an hour to reach the meeting place, set about filling in the intervening period.

Mr. Gormley's taste in literature ran to sentiment. He was a passionate devotee of Arabella Ann FitzHugh, an authoress who specialized in highly-coloured romances, and one of his reasons for visiting Middlethorpe that morning had been to secure from the library her latest novel. 'FitzHugh for Heart-throbs' across the jacket of a book was an irresistible lure to Mr. Gormley.

He became so absorbed in Miss FitzHugh's latest 'throbbing' that he was oblivious to the passing of time, and only realized that it was half-past eleven when he heard a clock in the village striking. Hurriedly he closed his book, rose to his feet, and putting on his shabby coat and cap crept out without disturbing the sleeping household.

The night was dark and a cold wind

was blowing fitfully. Mr. Gormley gave a little shiver and turned up his coat collar. Presently he came to a stile set in the thick hedge that bordered the road, and climbing this he struck off across open fields. It was near this point that he had heard the conversation between Alan Wargreave and Ilene Dinsley. Mr. Gormley was a confirmed 'snooper', and for a long time he had been aware of the secret meetings that had taken place between the girl and Lord Hillingdon's secretary. The memory of that conversation came to him now as he passed the place, and he wondered how it might be turned to his advantage. There were possibilities there. He would have to consider the matter carefully.

The narrow track he was following came to an end at another stile, and beyond this the black shape of his objective loomed dimly. It was a dilapidated and disused barn, standing in one corner of a hayfield. Mr. Gormley approached it, peering into the gloom to catch a glimpse of the man he had come to meet. But there was no sign of anyone, and a muttered curse rose to his lips. It must be already twelve o'clock. Was he going to be kept waiting?

And then he saw a shadow detach itself from the doorway.

'Is that Gormley?' said a voice softly.

'Yes,' answered Gormley.

'Well, I'm here,' said the other curtly. 'What do you want with me?'

'You know very well what I want,' said Mr. Gormley. 'I saw you kill Flood, and I want to know how much you're prepared to pay to keep my mouth shut.'

''I, said the fly',' murmured the man below his breath.

'What's that you say?' demanded Mr. Gormley.

'I was thinking of an old nursery rhyme,' answered the other.

''Who killed cock robin? I, said the sparrow, with my bow and arrow. Who saw him die? I, said the fly, with my little eye'.'

Mr. Gormley chuckled.

'Appropriate, ain't it?' he said.

'Very,' replied the murderer dryly. 'So you want money to keep silent, do you? How much?'

This was the point that had been worrying the blackmailer, and he hesitated.

'Come on, make your proposition!' said the unknown impatiently. 'I don't want to hang about here all night.'

'You'll stay as long as I want you to!' snapped Mr. Gormley. 'It's me who does the ordering, and don't you forget it! What about a thousand pounds?' The other gave a hard laugh.

'Why not make it a million?' he suggested. 'It's just as possible.'

'Oh, come now,' said Mr. Gormley. 'You can find a thousand if you want to.'

'How do you know that?' demanded the other.

'I'm sure you can,' said the wizened man. 'Ain't it worth a little effort? Don't forget, a word from me and you'd be in Queer Street.'

'A thousand pounds is impossible!' There was a definite note in the low voice. 'Quite out of the question. I'm prepared to pay you five pounds a week, but I can't pay you a penny more.'

Mr. Gormley thought rapidly. He was disappointed. He had expected to be able to squeeze more. But there was always Dinsley. He could add a bit to his demands there, and five pounds a week wasn't a bad income for nothing.

'Make it seven,' he said, and sensed rather than saw the other shake his head.

'Can't be done!' he replied briefly. 'Five pounds is the limit, and that 'ull be difficult enough.'

'Very well,' agreed Gormley reluctantly. 'How are you goin' to pay it?'

'In notes every Saturday morning,' was the answer. 'I'll send it by post.'

'Startin' from this Saturday,' said Gormley, and the man agreed. 'Well, see that you keep it up,' said the little man harshly. 'The first time you miss you'll find a policeman tapping you on the shoulder, and you know what that means.'

'You dirty little toad!' said the other contemptuously. 'I'd like to break every bone in your miserable little body!'

'I dare say you would,' said Mr. Gormley. 'But you can't see? You daren't! And hard words hurt no one. I've taken precautions. If anything happens to me, well — I've put it all down in writin' and deposited with my lawyers.'

'Which is very lucky for you,' said the man. 'I'd as soon kill you as I'd think of destroying vermin!'

'Instead of which you've got to pay me!' chuckled Gormley complacently. 'Now don't forget. Five quid every Saturday mornin' or the balloon goes up.' He peered at the shadowy figure curiously. 'Why did you kill Flood and Baldock?' he asked.

'That's my business!' was the terse reply. 'You're getting your pound of flesh, be content with that. Is there anything else? Because I want to be going.'

'No,' said Mr. Gormley, 'that's all. But don't you try any funny tricks, otherwise you're for it!'

The other made no reply, and turning, strode quickly away into the darkness, leaving Mr. Gormley standing alone.

He waited a moment or two and then began to retrace his steps.

The night's work had not been as profitable as he had anticipated, but that couldn't be helped. It was no good demanding more than his victim could manage. Dinsley would have to make up the deficit. He had plenty of money and could afford it, anyway.

The future looked very bright to Mr. Gormley as he shuffled rapidly back towards the cottage where he lived. On the morrow he would give his notice. There was a little place that he had had his eye on for some time; a pretty little house standing in a patch of garden, which was going for seven hundred. He would buy that and settle down to a life of ease and comfort.

His cunning brain mapped out a pleasant existence, and no premonition came to him that he was not destined to enjoy the fruits of his scheme.

As he let himself in with his key and cautiously climbed the stairs to his room he had no pre-knowledge of the fate that awaited him. The shabby apartment was in darkness and as he crossed the threshold and fumbled in his pocket for his matches a hand touched him on the shoulder.

He swung round with a gasp, but before he could utter a cry strong fingers closed round his skinny neck. He was lifted and flung across his narrow bed. A knee crushed his chest and the grip on his throat tightened. He tore desperately at the hands that were throttling him, and his thin body writhed. The darkness of the room grew darker yet. Lights flashed brilliantly before his bulging eyes. The blood hammered in his head and an agonizing pain pierced his lungs. He felt his senses ebbing, made a last desperate effort to claw away those murderous fingers, and suddenly went limp . . .

For a moment or two the strangler retained his grip to make sure, and then loosening his fingers, which had dug deeply into Mr. Gormley's stringy neck, he straightened up. He was breathing quickly and jerkily from his exertions, and for a little while he stood motionless to recover himself.

Then bending over the body he felt for the heart of his victim, assured himself that it was still, and turning swiftly to the window made his exit by the way he had come — down the ladder that rested against the sill.

Removing this he carried it carefully to

the place from whence he had taken it, and when this was done he let himself out noiselessly by the little gate and vanished into the blackness of the night.

17

Inspector Shadgold Arrives

The discovery of the murder was made by the woman who had let Mr. Gormley his room. She immediately communicated with Sergeant Akeman, who in turn rang up the police station at Middlethorpe.

Inspector Noyes, early astir to prepare for the inquest on Preston Flood, received the news with mixed feelings, and hurried over to take charge of the investigations.

A careful search revealed the method by which the murderer had gained admission to the cottage — the marks of a ladder were easily distinguishable below the window — but no other clue came to light, nor did an inspection of the dead man's effects provide any useful information.

Mr. Gormley had been a neat and methodical man, with a predilection for destroying everything in the nature of documents and there were no letters or other scraps of writing that might have provided a clue to the motive for his death.

The news of the fourth crime quickly spread through the inhabitants of West Dorling, and created something of a panic.

It was through the agency of the voluble Mrs. Jiffer that Trevor Lowe and Medlock heard of it, as in the case of Ollen.

'Strangled, 'e was,' said Mrs. Jiffer. 'And accordin' to what they say, an 'orrible sight! Poor Mrs. Boles got a terrible shock when she went to wake 'im, and I don't wonder, 'aving slept in the same 'ouse with a dead man.'

'You can't say we lack excitement,' remarked Tom Medlock when they had succeeded in getting rid of his garrulous housekeeper. 'Talk about the peace of the country!'

'It's certainly not very peaceful in this district,' agreed Lowe. His face was stern and his brows were drawn down over his grey eyes. 'There seems to be a very busy person at work.'

'It's a lunatic, if you ask me!' declared the reporter. 'It seems pretty evident now that the same man was responsible for killing Ollen.'

'Yes, that seems likely,' murmured the dramatist absently. 'What I'm wondering is whether he also killed Flood and Baldock.'

They had been on the point of finishing breakfast when Mrs. Jiffer had excitedly appeared with the news, and drinking his coffee he rose to his feet and began to fill his pipe.

'I can't say I'm altogether surprised about Gormley,' he remarked, pressing the tobacco carefully into the charred bowl. 'He was obviously playing a queer game. But what I don't quite see is where he fits in with the arrow business.'

'Is it possible,' suggested Medlock, lighting a cigarette, 'that Dinsley's at the bottom of the whole thing?'

'Meaning,' said his friend, 'that he killed Flood, Baldock, Ollen and Gormley?'

The reporter nodded.

'It's possible,' said Lowe. 'But I'm not altogether satisfied with that solution.'

'Why?' asked Medlock. 'It seems to me to be the most plausible. We know that in Gormley's case he had a motive, the man was blackmailing him, and he may have had an equally good motive so far as Flood and Baldock were concerned.'

'And what about Ollen?'

Medlock shrugged his shoulders.

'Well, what about Ollen?' he repeated. 'Maybe Ollen knew something, too.'

'You're forgetting,' said Lowe, 'how Flood and Baldock were killed, aren't you?'

'No, I'm not,' argued the reporter. 'There's no evidence that Dinsley couldn't have fired those arrows as well as anyone else.'

'There I agree with you,' said his companion. 'But that wasn't exactly my meaning. I'm not disputing the fact that Dinsley was quite capable, so far as we know, of using a bow. What I'm going on is the fact that I'm convinced the murders of Flood and Baldock were a surprise and a shock to him.'

'There's such a thing as being a good actor,' pointed out Medlock.

'If he was acting,' declared Lowe, 'then

he's the greatest actor the world has ever known.'

'Well, I can't see any other explanation,' grunted his friend. 'Who else is there who could be responsible?'

'What's the population of England?' said the dramatist with a wry smile.

'Meaning that anybody could,' said Medlock. 'Yes, I suppose you're right.'

'The whole thing,' Lowe went on, 'is very involved. At least involved on the surface because we are not in possession of one item of information that could possibly make everything clear. We have no knowledge, at present, of these men's past histories and that's where we've got to seek for a solution. What were they before they came to West Dorling? Why did they come to West Dorling? Who were their friends and enemies? We don't know. All we know is that a few months ago they came and settled in this district. We don't even know why they came. We don't know what secret Gormley held which enabled him to try and blackmail Dinsley.'

'Dinsley knows,' said Medlock meaningfully.

'Yes, and he's likely to keep his knowledge to himself!' retorted Lowe. 'You can depend upon it that *he's* not giving anything away.'

'Well, it looks pretty hopeless the way you put it,' muttered the reporter.

'At the present moment,' said his friend, 'it *is* hopeless. We're wasting time, Tom. We're trying to evolve a theory without sufficient data and it can't be done. The only way this crime will ever be solved is by patient investigation. That's why I'm rather glad the Chief Constable has decided to call in the aid of Scotland Yard. With their vast organization they can cover the ground much more quickly than the local police. We've got to go back to the beginning of things; to the unknown causes of which we've only seen the effects. And now we'd better be going unless we want to be late.'

The inquest on Preston Flood was being held in the schoolroom, and when they reached that ugly building they discovered a little knot of London Press men, the majority of whom knew Medlock and hailed him with delight.

Lowe sought out Inspector Noyes, and discovered that worried official talking to a dapper, grey-haired little man whom he introduced as Doctor Pritchard.

Doctor Pritchard came from Middle-thorpe and acted as coroner for the district. He was a pleasant man, without any of the bumptiousness that the dramatist had often found was characteristic of the country coroner.

'This is an extraordinary affair,' he remarked, 'and I don't think the inquiry this morning is going to make it any clearer.'

'You're asking for an adjournment, I suppose?' said Lowe, looking at Noyes, and the Inspector nodded.

'Yes, naturally, sir,' he replied.

'All we shall take,' said the coroner, 'is the medical evidence and the evidence of identification.'

'Are you including Baldock as well?' inquired the dramatist.

'Yes,' said Doctor Pritchard, 'it'll save a lot of time.' He shook his head. 'We're going to be fairly busy apparently,' he went on, 'There'll be an inquest on Ollen, and then this new murder — what's-his-name.'

'Gormley,' said Noyes. 'It's a regular epidemic, ain't it?'

'Did you discover anything likely to provide a clue to the murderer?' asked Lowe, and the Inspector shook his head.

'Not a thing,' he answered gloomily. 'Though I'm sure it was the same person as killed Ollen. The method of the crime was identical.'

'But Gormley was strangled, wasn't he?' said Lowe.

'Yes, sir,' answered Noyes. 'I don't mean that. I mean the ladder.'

'Oh, he used a ladder, did he?' said the dramatist.

'Yes, we found the marks under the window where it had stood,' replied Noyes. 'Only this time he must have climbed right into the room. It's my opinion that Gormley had been out and that the fellow who killed him concealed himself in the room and waited for him to come back.'

'What makes you think that?' asked Lowe.

'Well, sir,' said Noyes. 'Gormley had his coat on and his boots were covered in dust. His cap was lying on the floor where it had fallen when he was attacked.'

'So you think he'd been out,' murmured the dramatist thoughtfully. 'What time was the crime committed?'

'As near as Doctor Chambers can say, about half-past two.'

'H'm!' Lowe pursed his lips. 'As near as possible the same time as Ollen was killed,' he remarked. 'Queer time for Gormley to have been out. Wonder where he went?'

'Perhaps Mr. Dinsley could tell us that,' said Noyes significantly.

'You think he went to see Dinsley?'

'I do, sir!' declared the Inspector. 'And it wouldn't surprise me very much to know that Dinsley is the feller who choked the life out of him.'

'But I thought you had a man watching Dinsley?'

'So I have,' answered Noyes, 'and that's the trouble. My man swears that Dinsley didn't leave his house.'

'Well, in that case,' said Lowe, 'I don't see how he could have killed Gormley.'

'I'm not at all sure, sir,' said the Inspector, 'that my man's information is reliable.

Oh, I don't mean that he doesn't think he's speaking the truth, but how can he be sure? The only way, in my opinion, that anyone can be sure that Dinsley didn't leave his house last night was to have been with him, in his bedroom. My man was watching from outside, and it wouldn't take much cleverness on Dinsley's part for him to slip out unnoticed.'

'No I think you're right,' agreed Lowe, mentally picturing Highfield House and its surroundings. 'But at the same time you're up against a nasty snag if you ever pulled Dinsley in and accused him of the crime. Your man's evidence would go a long way to convince a jury that he couldn't have done it.'

'I know that,' said the Inspector pessimistically. 'However, I understand from the Chief Constable that they're sending down a man from the Yard this morning. Perhaps he'll be more successful. Anyway, the responsibility 'ull be off my shoulders.'

A few minutes later the inquest began. The proceedings were brief and not particularly illuminating. When the jury had been sworn and viewed the body, John Dinsley was called to give evidence of identification.

The thin man did so, in a low tremulous voice, and Lowe thought he looked ill and worried. There was nothing extraordinary in this since it was a natural outcome of the reason for his presence.

After him came Flood's butler, and then Doctor Chambers, who gave evidence of the cause of death. Inspector Noyes asked for and received a fortnight's adjournment pending further investigations on the part of the police. The inquiry into Flood's death then concluded, to be repeated practically verbatim in the case of Baldock.

The London Press men were obviously disappointed, and Lowe saw them grouped round Medlock as the bare schoolroom cleared. He was on the point of taking his own departure when a man came elbowing his way through the dispersing crowds of village sightseers; a short, thick-set man, with a florid face, on whose head was perched a hard derby hat.

He caught sight of the dramatist and his face lit with a smile of recognition.

'Hello, Mr. Lowe!' he grunted, coming over and holding out his hand. 'Just arrived. Hoped I'd be here in time for the inquest.'

'You're too late, Shadgold,' he said. 'But you haven't missed anything. It was the usual adjournment.' He turned to Noyes. 'This is Detective-Inspector Shadgold, of Scotland Yard.' He introduced the two men. 'Inspector Noyes, of the local police.'

'How d'you do, Inspector,' said Shadgold. 'Glad to meet you. Is there anywhere where we can go and have a talk? I know nothing about this business except what I've read in the newspaper reports.'

'We'll go back to the station,' said Noyes. 'The Chief Constable 'ull be there, I expect. You coming with us, Mr. Lowe?'

18

The Name on the List

'I'm glad,' remarked Trevor Lowe, 'that it was you they sent down, Shadgold.'

'Thank you, Mr. Lowe,' grunted the Inspector. 'I'm not at all sure that I am. It's a teaser. A regular tangle, so far as I can see.'

The long conference at Middlethorpe police station was over. Shadgold had listened to all the details concerning the murders with an increasing expression of gloom, and when he had noted all the important facts, and asked one or two questions, Lowe had suggested that he should return to Medlock's cottage for lunch.

The Inspector agreed with alacrity, and they were making their way slowly towards their destination.

'I'll admit,' said the dramatist, 'that it appears to be a difficult proposition, but

215

all the same it's remarkably interesting.'

'That may be,' retorted Shadgold. 'Personally I like something a little more plain sailing. What opinion have you formed?'

'I haven't formed any at the moment,' answered Lowe candidly. 'Before we can start forming opinions, Shadgold, we've got to collect a lot more information.'

'You're telling me!' growled the Inspector. 'You mean we've got to *start* collecting information! We haven't got any yet, so far as I can see.'

'No,' agreed his friend. 'But we've got three good leads. The first is, where did the arrows come from? You can't pick up those things in a department store, Shadgold. They're unique, and somebody made 'em. If we can find out who, we may be able to trace how they came into the possession of the murderer.'

'We've got that in hand now,' said the Inspector. 'Our expert says that they're probably of foreign manufacture. Venetian, most likely, and that they're very old. It'll take some time to trace 'em, even if we're successful at all. What's the second lead?'

'The second,' said Lowe, 'is the fact that the person who committed the murders — I'm talking now about Flood and Baldock — must be an expert at archery. I've already written to the Toxophilite Society asking for a list of their members during the past thirty years. Maybe that'll help. There are also a number of archery clubs throughout the country whose membership must be investigated.'

'That's going to take time, too,' grunted Shadgold. 'And supposing the killer isn't a member of an archery club, Mr. Lowe?'

'Well then we can't help it,' said Lowe, shrugging his shoulders. 'But it's worth trying. The third concerns Baldock, Flood and Dinsley before they came to West Dorling. What brought them together and what was their business? In fact who they were and all about them.'

'That's going to be about as easy as your other two,' grumbled Shadgold despondently. 'They've no criminal records, I suppose you know that already? Which means that we're going to have a devil of a job to trace 'em up.'

'Particularly,' said the dramatist, 'if, as I suspect, the names they were passing under here were not their real ones.'

'It's a great pity,' remarked the Inspector, 'that this fellow Gormley isn't alive. He might have been able to help us tremendously.'

Lowe disagreed with him.

'I don't think he *would*,' he answered, with emphasis on the 'would'. 'We tried to extract some information from him, and he was like an oyster. And I don't think you would have been any more successful. Obviously he considered it paid him to keep his mouth shut, and he kept it shut!'

'And now,' said Shadgold, 'somebody's shut it for him permanently. I'm inclined to agree with the Inspector here that Dinsley is the fellow we want.'

'He can certainly give you a great deal of information — if you can make him talk,' said Lowe. 'But the question is, can you? He maintains that he knew very little about Flood and Baldock, and there's nothing to prove he isn't speaking the truth. In fact all the evidence tends to confirm what he says. They scarcely ever spoke to each other and very seldom met. If Dinsley likes to keep silent he's in a very strong position. There's absolutely not a scrap of evidence to warrant his arrest. If you arrested him today you'd have to let him go tomorrow.'

'As I said, it's a teaser!' growled the Inspector, mopping his perspiring face. 'How much further is this place, Mr Lowe?'

'Only about half a mile now,' said the dramatist soothingly, and Shadgold sighed.

'I like your idea of a short walk,' he said sadly.

'The exercise 'ull do you good,' said Lowe. 'There's nothing like walking when you've got a knotty problem to chew over.'

Shadgold made no reply to this assertion, and they walked on in silence. When they eventually reached the cottage they found Medlock had not returned. There was, however, a message from him, which Mrs. Jiffer delivered. He was lunching in Middlethorpe and asked

Lowe to excuse him. He had met an old friend among the reporters who had come down.

The dramatist was not altogether sorry. It would give him a chance to talk things over with Shadgold in private. Medlock was a good fellow, but he was a reporter, and Lowe had no wish that anything he might suggest should receive premature publicity.

They had finished lunch when Mrs. Jiffer appeared with a bulky envelope. It had arrived by the second post, but she had forgotten to bring it in.

'I'm very sorry, sir,' she said, 'but I put it on the dresser and it clean went out of me mind.'

Lowe opened it and discovered, as he had expected, that it was from the secretary of the Toxophilite Society. It was against their rule to give a list of members, but considering the circumstances the committee had agreed to waive this point. At the same time the secretary hoped that Mr. Lowe would regard the information which was enclosed as entirely confidential.

The information enclosed consisted of a bulky wad of typewritten names and addresses.

'Well,' said the dramatist, when lunch had been cleared away and he had supplied Shadgold with a cigar and lit his own pipe, 'let's see if we're going to be lucky.'

He pulled up a chair and began conscientiously to go through the list. There were nearly fifty sheets, and it was not until he came to the fortieth that he discovered anything of interest, and then as his finger ran down the page he emitted a low whistle.

The Inspector, who was on the point of dropping asleep, sat up with a jerk.

'What is it?' he asked. 'Have you found something?'

Lowe nodded.

'I think I have,' he answered seriously. 'Look at this.'

Shadgold hoisted himself to his feet, came over to his side, and leaned forward.

'Lord Hillingdon,' he read. 'Dorling Manor, West Dorling. 104a, Berkley Street. Who's this fellow?' he demanded.

'He's a sort of 'Lord of the Manor' in these parts,' answered Lowe, and his eyes were thoughtful. 'So Lord Hillingdon is, or was, a member of the Toxophilite Society.'

'Which means that he understands archery, and he also lives in the district,' remarked Shadgold, his eyes gleaming. 'I think we've got hold of something, Mr. Lowe. Did he know Flood and Baldock?'

'He must have known of them,' said Lowe. 'This is worth following up.' He rose to his feet, and going into Tom Medlock's study picked up the telephone.

After a few minutes' delay he was connected with Middlethorpe police station and was speaking to Inspector Noyes.

'Can you come along?' he said. 'I think I've discovered something that may be useful.'

'I'll be with you in half an hour,' said Noyes, and Lowe returned to the dining room.

'I believe this may be very important,' he said, knocking the ashes out of his pipe and refilling it slowly. 'It suggests possibilities. Hillingdon is a very rich man. He and his family before him have lived in West Dorling for years. For some reason or other Dinsley, Baldock and Flood came to live in an out-of-the-way village like this eighteen months ago. And we know, or at least we have a strong suspicion, that they came for some purpose that was illegal, a purpose that I am inclined to think was known to Gormley. From some unknown source these three men drew a large income. It seems only reasonable to suppose that that source was local, since otherwise it was unnecessary for them to take up their residences here. Dinsley is certainly not, and Baldock and Flood were definitely not, the types of men who would choose to live in the country unless they were forced. The only rich man in the district is Hillingdon, and he is, or was, a member of the Toxophilite Society.'

He paused, struck a match, and lit his pipe.

'Yes,' he murmured. 'I think Hillingdon will be worth investigating.'

19

The Man Who Knew

There is, just before the junction of New Cross Gate and Deptford Broadway, a narrow little street that is distinguished from all the other narrow little streets in its immediate vicinity by the name Little Holland Street.

Its ancient houses consist, for the most part, of offices, and by the side of the narrow entrances can be seen boards and plates in various stages of dilapidation, bearing faded inscriptions.

Beside a narrow doorway on the right-hand side is a small brass tablet, green with corrosion and lack of polish, on which is the name 'Alfred Viness, Solicitor. Third Floor'.

If you take the trouble to climb the narrow and dirty staircase to the third floor you will come upon two doors facing you, one of which repeats the

224

inscription: 'Alfred Viness, Solicitor', with the additional word 'Private'; and the other bears merely one word: 'Inquiries'.

If, having reached so far, you are sufficiently curious to open this second door, you will find within a very small and very dusty office, inhabited solely by an academic-looking girl between seventeen and eighteen. This is Mr. Alfred Viness' sole staff.

Mr. Alfred Viness himself, if he so wishes, can be reached by passing through a communicating door covered with faded green baize. Mr. Viness' office is scarcely larger than the outer one and only a little less dirty.

A torn and ragged carpet partially covers the stained floor. A large, flat-topped writing table, littered with bundles of yellow papers, occupies the centre of the room. An ancient safe, an even older filing cabinet, and a series of shelves containing battered black boxes complete the entire furnishings.

Mr. Viness himself is in keeping with these rather unprepossessing surroundings. He is a small man with a baldish head and weak eyes. His nose is large and bulbous and of an unbeautiful colour which combines shades of red and purple with a tinge of blue. His short and ragged moustache is stained with the snuff of which he is an inveterate partaker, and his short, stubby hands are dirty and neglected.

In fact the whole of Mr. Viness' appearance suggests neglect, both physical and moral.

His practice is a peculiar one. To that dingy office come shabbily attired men and sometimes women, to pour into the ears of the lawyer details of their relations' latest delinquencies, and Mr. Viness will later appear in court and defend the unfortunate who has been caught shoplifting or 'wizzing' or, now and again, been brought up on some graver charge.

Mr. Viness is not a popular man with the police, for they have a strong suspicion that he gains more from his cases than his legitimate fee. Rumours have been circulated, without, it is true, any tangible proof, that on one or two occasions stolen property has mysteriously disappeared when the Little Holland Street lawyer has been handling the robber's defence. These malicious rumours have even reached the ears of Mr. Viness himself, but he is impervious to slander, or at any rate it troubles him very little, for he merely takes a larger pinch of snuff and smiles, revealing his yellow and broken teeth. 'Hard words,' as he once remarked to an irate Inspector, 'hurt no one.' And certainly there was no falling off in his business.

On the morning following the inquest at West Dorling he sat in his shabby room thoughtfully picking his teeth and eyeing the closely written document that lay spread on the dirty blotting-pad before him. It was penned in small and crabbed writing and was indeed the document that Mr. Gormley, in his efforts to safeguard himself, had so laboriously compiled.

Mr. Viness had read in his evening paper of the murder of his client, and immediately on arriving at his office had unlocked his safe and produced the envelope, which had been committed to his care. His reaction when he had digested the contents was peculiar, considering his profession. As a man of law it was clearly his duty to act on the information that it contained, for here was a clear and concise account of the murder of Preston Flood, an eyewitness's account, with the name of the murderer in black and white.

It would have been natural to suppose, under the circumstances, that Mr. Viness would immediately get in touch with the police, but, curiously enough, he did nothing of the sort.

He read the statement carefully through for the third time, and settling himself in his padded chair stared with narrow eyes at the dirty inkstand. The covering letter which had accompanied the statement plainly said that in the event of the writer's death Mr. Viness was to forward the enclosed document to the police. But the lawyer was in no hurry to carry out these instructions. In fact he had almost quite made up his mind not to do anything of the sort. There was no particular affection between himself and the official force, and so far as profits went he would gain nothing by seeing the murderer of Preston Flood arrested.

He stretched out his hand, lifted a box from his table, opened it, and inserting a finger and thumb withdrew a pinch of brown powder, which he applied to each nostril and sniffed contentedly.

With his head considerably clearer he once more examined the position. He was in possession of very valuable knowledge, valuable so long as he kept it to himself. Once it reached the police it was no longer an asset. He held in his hand the life of the man who had killed Preston Flood and, obviously of course, Baldock. How much was that life worth to its owner? Evidently all he possessed. Money was no good to a man who was buried in quicklime.

Mr. Viness saw possibilities of securing quite a comfortable addition to his already large banking account, and with no risk to himself. That he was contemplating breaking the law troubled him not at all. He had broken the law of which he was a representative too often to have any qualms of conscience about it. Providing he could do so with impunity and without risk to himself, he was prepared to continue breaking the law. That was the only thing that was giving him any cause for worry. By doing what he contemplated he was making himself an accessory to two murders, possibly three, for he had little doubt that the man who had killed Gormley was the man mentioned in the statement. Now, was there any likelihood of this coming to light? He could see very little. The man he was considering blackmailing would, for obvious reasons, never give him away, for although it might mean a term of imprisonment for Mr. Viness it meant death for him.

So far as he could see there was no possible risk.

He picked up the sheets of paper and slowly read them through again. The document was unwitnessed, but that could easily be put right. He pressed a button.

The slatternly girl, after some delay, answered the summons.

'You remember that gentleman who came the other day,' said her employer, 'and signed a statement?'

'Which gentleman?' asked the girl.

'The gentleman who came, when was it? Friday afternoon,' said Mr. Viness.

'I don't remember who you mean,' she answered.

'I called you in to witness a statement,' he said impatiently, 'and you forgot to sign it.' He was on safe ground, for her memory was not of the best, and so many 'gentlemen' called with statements that required witnessing that it was doubtful if she would remember one way or the other. 'Anyway, it doesn't matter. You can sign your name now. Only if you're asked you'll have to say you did it in his presence, you understand?'

She nodded. She was not very bright. Her father had killed her mother just after her birth in a drunken frenzy and was still serving a sentence for manslaughter.

Mr. Viness took a pen, covered the writing with a sheet of paper, and pointed to a blank space.

'Sign your name there,' he ordered, and she complied.

When she had gone back to the outer

office he waited for the signature to dry and examined the document again complacently.

Everything was now legally in order. He had a definite statement, signed and witnessed, which could be produced at any moment to put a rope round the neck of the man mentioned in it.

He unfolded it carefully, went over to his safe, unlocked it, put the document inside, and closed the door, relocking it and returning the key to his pocket. All he had to do now was to make up his mind as to the best method of approach.

He took another pinch of snuff to help his decision and presently decided on making a personal call. Writing was dangerous; telephone messages could be listened in to. A personal interview, without witnesses, was safe.

He took from a drawer of his desk a timetable and looked up the trains. There was no station at West Dorling. The nearest was Middlethorpe. There was a train that afternoon that would land him at his destination just after six. It would be best to do what he had to do under cover of darkness, which meant that he would have to while away several hours somewhere. That wouldn't be difficult.

Once more he called in his clerk.

'I shall be leaving at three,' he said. 'I'm going out of town to interview a client. You can put off any appointments I have this afternoon until tomorrow. Leave at the usual time.'

She nodded, and for the rest of the morning he devoted himself to his normal routine of work. After his frugal lunch of sandwiches, which he ate in the office, washed down by a stiff whisky and soda, he locked his desk, put on his shabby overcoat, and prepared to depart.

'I shall be in at the usual time in the morning,' he said as he passed through the outer office, and firmly believed what he said.

But he was not there at the usual time, neither did he ever return to the office again. Mr. Viness, like a great many clever men, had made the fatal mistake of overestimating his own acumen.

20

The Interview

Inspector Noyes lay back in one of Tom Medlock's comfortable easy chairs and emitted a strange series of grunts, gasps, and hisses.

'It's certainly a queer coincidence, Mr. Lowe,' he bellowed. 'But I don't think it can be anything more. It's impossible that his lordship can be mixed up in this business.'

'Why?' demanded Shadgold.

'Well — 'The direct question found the Inspector momentarily nonplussed. 'I just can't credit it.'

'That doesn't make it impossible,' said Lowe quietly. 'I think, Inspector, that you're rather allowing your very natural prejudices to bias you. Lord Hillingdon is practically a national institution in West Dorling. Isn't it rather a case of 'The king can do no wrong'?'

The Inspector's face went a little redder than its natural colour.

'Well, I suppose when you put it like that, sir,' he admitted reluctantly, 'there is something in what you say.'

'It's quite understandable,' said the dramatist. 'You were born and bred in the district and you look upon Lord Hillingdon as a kind of — well, if not exactly a deity, very nearly. But apart from that what do you really know about him?'

'You're quite right, Mr. Lowe, I don't know anything, except what's general knowledge. At the same time it'll take a lot to convince me that he's a murderer.'

'Well, we haven't got as far as accusing him yet!' grunted Shadgold. 'All we're doing at present is trying to find out the person responsible. We were hoping you would help us.'

Noyes' expression was doubtful.

'I really know very little — '

'Well, tell us what you do know,' said Lowe. 'What sort of man is Hillingdon?'

'A very nice gentleman!' declared the Inspector emphatically. 'One of the old kind, and you don't find many of 'em these days. Generous and just, like his father afore him.'

'How long has he held the title?' asked the dramatist.

'Since just after the war,' answered Noyes.

'He's married, of course?' continued Lowe.

'Yes. The present Lady Hillingdon is his second wife. His first wife died. There was some trouble there.'

'Oh?' said the dramatist. 'What kind of trouble?'

'I'm not rightly sure of the facts,' replied Noyes. 'But I believed the old earl disapproved and there was a row between them. You see, Lord Hillingdon was a young man then, and his first wife was an actress I think. She died, I understand, just before the War.'

'And he married again?' said Shadgold, and Noyes nodded.

'Yes. He married the eldest daughter of the Earl of Whitsey. As nice a lady as you'd wish to meet. A beautiful girl she was then.'

'Any children?' said the dramatist.

'One son,' answered the Inspector. 'He's at Oxford now. A nice young feller.'

'Well, there doesn't seem to be

anything there that might help us,' said Lowe thoughtfully. 'Did he know Flood or the others?'

'I couldn't say that,' said Noyes shaking his head. 'I shouldn't think it was likely. If you'll excuse me saying so I think you're both wasting your time over Lord Hillingdon.'

'You may quite possibly be right,' said Lowe. 'At the same time we've got to follow up every possible line. The man who killed these two was an expert in archery, and at the present moment the only man in the district who could be described as such is Lord Hillingdon. Can you think of anything else that might be worth noting?'

Noyes screwed up his face and after a pause shook his head.

'No, I can't, and that's a fact!' he declared. 'There's nothing — ' He stopped suddenly. 'Well, there is, one thing, but I don't suppose it's got anything to do with what we're talking about.'

'Well, let's hear it, anyway,' said the dramatist encouragingly.

'There was an attempted robbery at the Manor, let me see, it 'ud be eighteen months ago now,' said the Inspector slowly. 'Somebody broke in, but nothin' was stolen. They awakened Lord Hillingdon before they could do any damage, and he came down and, I believe, shot at the burglar. Anyway, he didn't hit him. All the damage he did was to make a hole in one of the pictures. A valuable paintin', too, I believe.'

'The burglar wasn't caught?' said Trevor Lowe, and Noyes shook his head.

'Eighteen months ago,' murmured the dramatist. 'That 'ud be just before these three men came to live in the district.'

'That's right, sir,' said the Inspector.

Lowe rubbed his chin thoughtfully.

'H'm! Well, as you say, there may be no connection. I still think,' — he turned to Shadgold — 'it would do no harm if you found out everything possible concerning Hillingdon. Try back to this first marriage of his. Find out who it was he married and under what circumstances she died.'

'I'll get on to that right away,' said Shadgold, and picked up the telephone.

In a few seconds he was connected with the Yard and had issued brief instructions to the inquiry department. Shortly afterward Noyes took his departure, still apparently convinced that they were following an unprofitable line of inquiry.

The man they had been discussing was, at that moment, standing in a telephone booth speaking to John Dinsley.

'I *must* see you!' There was an urgent note in Hillingdon's voice. 'It's imperative! Can you meet me somewhere?'

There was a pause, and then the man at the other end of the wire replied.

'You know Elmer Lane . . . ? Well, walk along until you come to the stile on the right that leads to Briarthorpe Farm. I'll join you there as soon as possible.'

There was a click as the receiver was hung up, and Lord Hillingdon came out of the call box and glanced quickly about him. There was nobody in sight, and he moved off down the High Street in the direction of the said meeting place.

His face was pale and there were dark shadows under his eyes. He looked like a man who had slept badly, and this was but the truth. Ever since he had heard of the murders he had been restless and uneasy. Again and again he had tried to screw up his courage and arrange this interview with the one man who could set his fears at rest, and again and again he had found himself unable to take the initial steps. Now that it was done he wondered whether it had been a false move. And yet he must know, he must find out for his own peace of mind, whether there was anything that could possibly give publicity to the secret that he had striven so long to keep hidden.

He turned into the narrow opening of Elmer Lane and followed its twisting course until he reached the stile Dinsley had mentioned.

It was half an hour before the tall figure of Dinsley came into sight. The man's thin face was haggard, and he looked almost as worried as Hillingdon.

'What did you want to see me about?' he asked impatiently, as he came within speaking distance.

'I *had* to see you,' answered Hillingdon. 'It's about Flood and Baldock.'

Dinsley surveyed him coldly and suspiciously.

'What about them?' he demanded.

'What difference does it make — their dying as they did?' muttered Hillingdon.

'Difference? It makes no difference. You'll pay the money just the same!'

'I wasn't thinking about that.' The old man cleared his throat. 'I was thinking — did they — was there anything among their effects that's likely — '

'Oh, I see!' Dinsley broke in with a sneer. 'You were wondering whether the police would unearth anything about you. Well, you can set your mind at rest. There was nothing.'

Hillingdon uttered a sigh of relief.

'It's been worrying me terribly,' he confessed. 'I was afraid — that it might come out.'

'I'm glad you suggested this interview, anyway,' said Dinsley, 'because I wanted to see you. I've got to alter my plans. I'm going away. So instead of the original arrangement I shall want a lump sum. I think fifty thousand pounds 'ull meet the case.'

Hillingdon stared at him, aghast at the demand.

'It's impossible!' he answered.

'Is it?' snapped Dinsley. 'Well you'd better make it possible. That's the amount I want, and I want it before the end of the week!'

'But I can't possibly manage it!' protested Hillingdon. 'I haven't fifty thousand pounds in fluid cash!'

'I don't mind how you get it,' interrupted the other gruffly. 'All I know is I want it, and if you don't find it you can take the consequences. There's a reporter in this village and I've no doubt I could give him information that 'ud make his mouth water.'

'I daresay the amount could be found.' Hillingdon licked his dry lips. 'But not in the time. You must give me longer. I should have to sell certain shares.'

'I must have it by the end of the week!' persisted Dinsley. 'There are dozens of ways you can get it if you want to. Why sell shares? If you haven't got the ready cash there's any number of moneylenders who would fall over themselves to let you have it. After all, what's fifty thousand pounds compared with a scandal? My silence is cheap at the price.'

'I'll do what I can,' said Hillingdon. 'But you must be reasonable. I could raise half the amount by the end of the week and the remainder a fortnight later.'

'No good!' said Dinsley. 'I can't say where I'll be in a fortnight's time. I want the lot, or I shall have something to tell that reporter.' He gave a hard laugh. 'It 'ud make the sparks fly, wouldn't it? Can you imagine the sensation? 'Lord Hillingdon arrested for Bigamy? Heir to Earldom illegitmate!' It 'ud make nice reading for some of your friends.'

The old man gave a groan.

'Don't!' he whispered huskily. 'I didn't know. I was under the impression that my first wife was dead; I'd no idea she was alive . . .'

'That 'ud be a good defence, and it might make a difference to your sentence,' sneered Dinsley. 'But it wouldn't affect your wife's position, or your son's!'

He had touched upon the real fear that had brought that haunted look to Hillingdon's eyes; the dread that was ever present night and day, the dread that seeped into his dreams and brought him to shivering wakefulness in the silent hours, the cold sweat on his forehead. His son! The boy he worshipped was nameless, legally prohibited from carrying on the line.

'It must never become known!' he muttered. 'Never! I would do anything to prevent such a catastrophe!'

'Well, all you've got to do is to find fifty thousand pounds,' said Dinsley. 'I shall be here at six o'clock on Saturday night and I shall expect you to meet me with the money. In cash!' he added. 'A cheque will be no use to me.'

'Very well,' said the old man brokenly. 'I'll arrange it somehow.'

'You'd better!' snapped Dinsley, and turning on his heels he walked away without another word.

Hillingdon stared after him, his hands clenched until the knuckles showed white under the stretched skin; and then, with something that was almost a sob, he moved away, walking with the gait of a broken man.

21

Dinsley Decides to Quit

John Dinsley walked slowly back towards his house, taking the short cut across the fields by which he had come; and the man who lurked behind him, using every available cover to conceal his presence, followed in his wake.

The watcher put on to keep an eye on his movements by Inspector Noyes had witnessed the interview, although circumstances had forced him to keep too far away to overhear what had passed. He had seen the expression on Lord Hillingdon's face, however, and it had been sufficient to assure him that the meeting had not been a friendly one.

Unaware of the existence of the trailer, Dinsley continued on his way, his thoughts both pleasant and otherwise. It had taken him some time to make up his mind, but now that he had reached a decision he considered he was wise. There were trouble clouds brewing and he had always avoided trouble. With fifty thousand pounds he could clear out of the country before the storm burst. It was a respectable sum, and the knowledge that it would be in his possession by the end of the week was a pleasant thought. The unpleasant side concerned his own immediate position. He was aware that the police were suspicious, and only he knew what justification they had; but it was not only the police who worried him, it was the other — the slayer of his two associates. The dread of that unknown nemesis overshadowed his fear of the law. Had his schemes ended with the death of Flood or Baldock, or was he even now planning to add a third victim — Dinsley himself?

Looked at from every angle it was safer to go while the going was good. He had planned his getaway. He would leave West Dorling in the night, travel by hired car to London, and from thence to Southampton. A very slight disguise would be sufficient to render him unrecognizable,

246

and he could book a passage on one of the liners under an assumed name.

He reached his house, let himself in, and making his way to his study poured himself out a drink. He felt the need of an artificial stimulant these days, although he was an abstemious man.

There was no longer anything to worry about concerning Gormley. That was not only a relief, but it meant an appreciable saving.

He sat down at his desk with a pencil to plan his getaway. Perhaps it would be better if he took more elaborate precautions. He leaned back, tapping his teeth. His flight would naturally consolidate any suspicion there might be concerning him, and a hue and cry would be immediate. He would be wiser to give a little more thought to this. His original idea was too simple, too easily traceable. There was a swifter method of travel, which he had overlooked. The air!

He could charter a special 'plane which would land him in France almost before it was discovered he was gone. And once there it would surely not be difficult to

247

disappear completely.

He rang the bell and gave an order for his dinner to be served in the study. When it had been brought and he had eaten it he settled down to complete his plans.

It was late when he went up to bed, and when he had undressed he switched out the light and stood for some time looking out of the window into the darkness of the night. It was very dark indeed. He could see little except the dim outline of the trees and the long smudge that marked the shrubbery. After a moment or two he pulled the curtains and got into bed . . .

The watcher outside saw his light go out and sighed. It was not a particularly enviable job lurking about in the darkness, watching a house in which other people were sleeping soundly.

The cracked bell of the village clock struck one, and Detective Constable Higson turned up the collar of his coat and thrust his hands deeper into his pockets. It was getting chilly and he was fed up. Eight hours of this was enough to make any man fed up.

He wondered if he dared risk a smoke, and decided after a searching glance at the dark house that there was no reason why he shouldn't. Everybody had gone to bed and, being sensible people, were likely to remain there until the morning.

He pulled out a packet of cigarettes, stuck one between his lips, produced a tinder-lighter, and striking a spark cupped the glowing wick in his hands. The cigarette was something to be going on with, anyway. He inhaled the smoke gratefully. Only another two hours and then he was free until eleven o'clock when he supposed the whole weary business would start all over again.

If the Inspector thought this man Dinsley would bolt why didn't he arrest him? What was the sense in keeping a man out of bed to watch for something that never happened?

He finished his cigarette and yawned, moved over to the trunk of a tree, and leaning against it folded his arms. He found himself dozing and jerked himself to wakefulness. Not that it would matter much if he slept. There was not a living thing stirring anywhere near. However, it would be just his luck if something did happen while he was taking forty winks, and if it did he'd have a hell of a time explaining it away to Noyes.

It seemed more like six hours than two before he heard the welcome sound of the clock strike three, and he moved slowly down the drive towards the wide gate where he had arranged to meet his relief.

The man was punctual. As he came out into the roadway he heard his step approaching and presently he joined him.

'Anything happened?'

Higson shook his head.

'No. Nothin' likely to happen. The old beggar is fast asleep. Anything happen while you was on duty?'

'He went out,' said the other man, 'and met Lord Hillingdon in Elmer Lane. Not very friendly they wasn't, neither. I couldn't get close enough to 'ear what they was talkin' about, but you could tell that.'

'That's queer,' said Higson. 'Shouldn't have thought 'illingdon would have had much in common with a feller like Dinsley.'

'No, you wouldn't, would yer,' said his confrère. 'Anyway, they met. And the Inspector was pretty interested when I made me report. Seemed to regard it as important.'

'What's your opinion?' said Higson. 'D'you think this feller Dinsley did these murders?'

'No. And I don't think the Inspector thinks so, neither,' answered the other.

'Then what's the idea of keeping him under observation?' demanded Higson. 'If they don't think 'e's guilty why bother to have the place watched?'

'It's no good asking me.' The other man shrugged his shoulders. 'I ain't in Noyes' confidences.'

'Well, it seems stupid to me,' grunted Higson. 'Anyway, you've got it for the next eight hours, and I wish you joy. I'm goin' home.'

'All right. Don't be late in the mornin',' said his friend, and with a muttered 'good night' Higson left him and made his way hastily towards the station house.

Sergeant Akeman looked up as he entered the tiny charge room.

'Hello!' he said. 'Come to sign off?'

'Yes,' said Higson, 'and mighty glad, too. I've struck some jobs since I joined the force, but this is about the worst ever. Blinkin' cold and nothin' to see but darkness. I shall be glad of a bite to eat and a good sleep.'

He scribbled his name on the paper the sergeant pushed towards him, nodded a good night, and went to collect his bicycle.

He lived in one of a row of small cottages midway between West Dorling and Middlethorpe, and as he pedalled swiftly along the silent country road, his oil lamp casting a dim, flickering circle of light in front of him, his one thought was of food and sleep.

It was sheer accident that caused him to make his discovery. He had covered half the distance he had to go when, without warning, there was a sudden plop, followed by a sharp hissing, and the smooth running of the bicycle changed to an uneven bumping.

Higson swore beneath his breath and dismounted.

There was nothing for it but to continue his journey on foot, and after pausing to light a cigarette he set off, trundling his machine beside him. A few yards further on the narrow road turned into an S shaped bend, and as he came to the first of the rather sharp corners the light of his lamp fell on something that was lying on the grass strip that bordered the right-hand side of the road at this point.

Higson stopped and stared. The object was a man, and he appeared to be asleep. A tramp, probably, thought the detective, and moving over he stirred the motionless figure with his foot.

'Here, wake up,' he said. 'You can't — '

He stopped abruptly and his jaw dropped, for on the white face was something red and wet which gleamed in the dim light from the bicycle lamp.

With a swift intake of his breath Higson laid the machine down quickly, pulled an electric torch from his pocket, and directed its brighter beam on the thing by the roadside. In the clear circle of light he saw a medium-sized man, rather shabbily dressed. He lay on his side, but with his head turned towards the dark sky. There was blood on his face and on the front of his coat. Blood, too, on the grass on which he lay . . .

Higson peered at the upturned face and saw that it was a stranger.

' 'Ere's a rummy go!' he muttered in consternation. 'Another murder by the look of things. I wonder who 'e is?'

He had never seen Mr. Alfred Viness or he wouldn't have needed to ask that question.

22

The Burglary

Doctor Chambers rose wearily to his feet and brushed the knees of his trousers.

'He's been stabbed,' he said. 'And I should say he's been dead for about a couple of hours. How much more of this are we going to have?'

Inspector Noyes shook his head helplessly.

'Don't ask me, sir,' he replied. 'It's getting shocking.'

Inspector Shadgold uttered a grunt that might have meant anything.

'Who is the man?' he demanded.

'I don't know,' said Noyes. 'He's a stranger to me, and a stranger to the district. Maybe we'll find out when we search the pockets.'

He knelt down beside the motionless figure and began his examination. Shadgold and Lowe stood by him, watching.

Higson, after making the discovery, had hurried back to the police station at West Dorling, from whence a telephone message had been sent to Middlethorpe, and Inspector Noyes aroused. The Inspector had called for Lowe and Shadgold on his way. The Scotland Yard man, on Medlock's invitation, had taken up his abode at the reporter's cottage during his stay in the neighbourhood. The reporter himself had missed the latest sensation. He had telephoned later that afternoon saying he was going up to Town to see Mr. Bishop, the news editor, and would not be back that night.

By the light of the two lanterns held by Higson and the constable whom he had brought with him, Noyes ran through the contents of the pockets. Presently he looked up.

'This is the fellow, I think,' he said, consulting an open wallet. 'Alfred Viness.'

Shadgold uttered an exclamation.

'Viness! What's his address?'

'20, Little Holland Street, Deptford, according to the letters in this notecase,' said the Inspector. 'D'you know him?'

'I know him very well,' grunted the Inspector. 'He's a crook solicitor. He's been suspected for a long time of being a fence. What the deuce can he be doing here?'

'Perhaps,' suggested Trevor Lowe, 'the letters will answer that question.'

But they didn't. There were only three of them. Two were bills and the third was a request for an appointment by someone who signed himself 'Joe Bates'. There was nothing to suggest a reason for the dead lawyer's presence in West Dorling.

'It's mad!' said Shadgold. 'Sheer, crazy insanity! People round here get killed for no reason at all!'

'I'm beginning to think the same,' grunted Noyes despondently.

'Nothing ever happens without a reason,' said Lowe quietly. 'Is there anything else in the pockets, Inspector?'

Noyes continued his search and brought to light a handkerchief, some loose change, a watch and a battered cigarette case.

'Queer!' murmured the dramatist, when these were exhibited to him.

'Queer! I should say is was queer!'

growled Shadgold.

'I'm referring to the contents of the pockets,' explained Lowe.

'There's nothing very queer about them,' said the Inspector. 'What d'you mean?'

'I mean there are no keys,' said Lowe. 'Surely there should have been something of the sort, if it was only a latch key.'

'Yes, you're right, sir.' Noyes nodded. 'As you say, it's queer.'

'The man may quite possibly not have been carrying his keys,' said Lowe. 'But I think it's more than likely he was, and that the murderer took them away.'

'What for?' grunted Shadgold.

'Well, what does one generally want keys for?' said the dramatist with a faint smile, and the Scotland Yard man flushed.

'I don't mean that!' he retorted. 'You know very well what I mean.'

'I should say,' said Lowe thoughtfully, 'that he was after something this man had in his possession, and he's taken the keys in order to get it. You say the police suspected him of being a fence?'

Shadgold nodded.

'Yes. He had a very bad reputation,' he

answered. 'We've never been able to hang anything on him, but it was generally believed that when a man was caught after a robbery Viness would defend him on condition that the stolen property was turned over to him at a small price.'

'I see,' said the dramatist thoughtfully. 'Well, I think it would be a good idea if you got on to the Yard and suggested that they got in touch with the Deptford police and have this man's office searched. It may throw some light on his death.'

Doctor Chambers, an interested listener, stepped into the light.

'There's nothing more for me to do,' he said, 'so if you don't mind I'll be going. This is a straightforward killing, anyway. There are no glass arrows or other frills. It's just a downright stabbing!'

'Like Ollen,' said Noyes.

The doctor nodded.

'Yes, but it wasn't done with the same weapon,' he answered. 'This was a much thinner-bladed knife.'

'Our friend, if the same man's responsible, seems to believe in variety,' remarked Lowe.

'Do you think the same man's responsible, sir?' asked Noyes.

'I don't know,' confessed the dramatist. 'To be perfectly candid, I've never been implicated in a case so completely lacking in form! What I mean,' he hastened to explain as he saw the Inspector's puzzled frown, 'is that there's no coherence about it. It jumps all over the place.'

'Don't I know it!' said Noyes gloomily. 'If you ask me, I doubt whether we'll ever get to the bottom of it.'

The police photographers arrived at that moment, and he turned away to meet them. Presently there was a series of dull explosions and flashes as they took flashlight photographs of the body from various angles.

It was getting light when the remains of Mr. Viness were finally lifted on to an ambulance and carried away to the mortuary.

Lowe and Shadgold went back to Medlock's cottage, puzzled and thoughtful. Mrs. Jiffer was still sleeping, and the dramatist made some tea in the spotless kitchen and carried it into the study.

'It's not much use going back to bed,' he said. 'It's half past five already.'

The Inspector yawned.

'No, I suppose not,' he agreed. 'I'll have a word with the Yard.'

There was some delay in getting his connection, but eventually he was speaking to the night officer in charge. It was a long conversation, and when he hung up the receiver he gave a grunt of satisfaction.

'Well, that's that!' he remarked. 'They're getting in touch with the Deptford police and ringing me back. How the deuce do you think this fellow comes into it, Mr. Lowe?'

His friend shrugged his shoulders.

'I don't know!' he declared. 'I'm completely at sea. I haven't the least idea what is behind all this business or who is responsible, and that's the truth!'

'What do you make of this interview between Hillingdon and Dinsley?' said Shadgold, for they had been notified of the watcher's report.

'I think it tends to show,' said Lowe, 'that Hillingdon is mixed up in it. What we lack is information. That's been the whole trouble from the beginning. We can't get hold of anything concrete. If only we knew something about Flood and Baldock prior to their setting in the district we might have something to go on. But we don't. We don't know what Gormley knew.'

'In fact,' grunted Shadgold as he paused, 'we don't know anything except that five men have been killed.'

'That's the situation in a nutshell,' agreed Lowe. 'And we're not even in the position to say that they were killed by the same man. It's exasperating!'

'I can think of another word,' said the Inspector, 'which describes it even better!'

'Let's keep the party clean,' murmured Lowe. He took out his pipe, filled it, and lit it carefully. 'Now,' he said, 'let's see just where we stand. What we want to know is:

1. What brought Dinsley and Flood and Baldock to West Dorling, and where did the money come from to enable them to live in the style they kept up?

2. What did Gormley know that enabled him to threaten Dinsley with blackmail?

3. Why were Baldock and Flood killed with glass arrows?

4. Was the murder of Ollen a crime that has no connection with the main problem at all, or was it part and parcel of the original scheme?

5. Was Lord Hillingdon the man who killed Baldock and Flood, and was he also the source from which they obtained their money?

6. What hold had they over him in order to make him pay up, if it was his money they were living on?

7. What brought Viness to West Dorling?

8. Who was the archer?

Shadgold ran his fingers through his hair.

'And if we could find the answer to the last,' he said, 'it would probably clear up all the others.' He gave a prodigious yawn and rubbed his tired eyes. 'Well, we can't do more than we're doing,' he grunted.

'We've just got to wait as patiently as possible until some information comes through.'

The first came shortly after they had finished breakfast. The telephone bell rang and a voice inquired for Inspector Shadgold. Lowe, who had answered the summons, handed the instrument to the Scotland Yard man, and when he had taken the call he turned to the dramatist.

'You were right about those keys,' he said. 'The Deptford police went round to Viness' office and notified the Yard that the place was ransacked during the night, the safe opened, and a quantity of papers burned in the grate. I don't know that it gets us any farther though.'

'Every item of information gets us farther,' said Lowe. 'What we want to know mostly at the moment is something concerning the past history of Baldock, Flood and Dinsley.'

23

The First Clue

Tom Medlock returned just before midday and he was both amazed and delighted to hear the news of the latest sensational discovery.

'I'm already the envy of every reporter in The Street,' he declared with a chuckle. 'This 'ull make 'em go green! Tell me all the details.'

Lowe eyed him critically.

'Don't overdo it, Tom,' he warned, for his friend's face was pale and there were haggard lines about his mouth, which suggested he was using himself up rather badly. 'Remember you're a sick man.'

'I don't care if I'm a dead one!' declared Medlock obstinately.

He waited long enough for the dramatist to tell him briefly what he knew, and then dashed away to find Inspector Noyes and augment his scanty information.

Shadgold had gone over to Middlethorpe to see the Chief Constable soon
after the news of the robbery at Viness'
office had reached him, and Lowe was left
alone.

He was rather glad of the opportunity
offered for a little quiet thinking. From
his point of view the whole thing was very
unsatisfactory. He was no nearer to a
solution than he had been when he stood
looking down at the dead body of Preston
Flood in the ruins of Claydon Abbey.
Never had he been faced with such a
blank wall, such a dearth of material on
which to work. And yet, in the beginning,
the discovery of the murderer had not
looked to be such a formidable task. The
use of such a strange weapon as a glass
arrow had suggested that it would not be
difficult to find both its origin and its
user. It was true the inquiries then being
undertaken by Scotland Yard were only in
their infancy and in time would probably
yield results. But what rankled with Lowe
was his own inability to provide a ray of
daylight for himself.

The whole thing, he was convinced,

could be boiled down to one question. Why had the murderer chosen such a unique weapon?

In this he felt sure lay the answer to the problem, and for the life of him he couldn't conjecture. He had racked his brains until his head ached to find a reasonable explanation without result. Once that was clear he felt that everything else would drop automatically into place.

It was exasperating! He knocked the ashes out of his pipe savagely. Where was one to begin? Was there anything in the Hillingdon idea? There was that interview with Dinsley on the previous afternoon, which rather looked as though there might be. Assuming that the source of the money which had enabled these three men to live so extravagantly was Hillingdon, what hold had they on him?

Noyes had pooh-poohed the suggestion that he could have had anything to do with the affair, but then Noyes was prejudiced. He had been born and bred in the district, and to him Hillingdon was a king who could do no wrong. But Hillingdon had gone to meet Dinsley secretly, and he was, or had been, a member of the Toxophilite Society.

Lowe came to a sudden decision. He scribbled two notes, one for Medlock and one for Shadgold, briefly stating that he had gone to London and would be back either late that night or first thing in the morning. He gave these into the care of the surprised Mrs. Jiffer and got into his car.

At four o'clock that afternoon he was sitting in the smoking room of an exclusive club in Piccadilly, of which he was a member, having tea and keeping a sharp look-out for a certain man whom he had come there specially to meet. Brigadier General Sir Crayley-Watson was an inveterate gossip and one of the most crashing bores Lowe had ever met. As a general rule he studiously avoided him, as did the majority of the members. This afternoon, however, he was particularly anxious to see him. The white-haired, choleric old man knew everybody, and could produce at a moment's notice the full details of their past history, their present business, and their possible future. He had the latest scandal at his fingertips, and was a mine of information concerning everyone and everything.

He usually occupied a chair in one of the windows, which, from long use, was more or less tacitly regarded as his especial property. But this afternoon the chair was empty. By one of those perverse tricks of fate the man he had come to see was absent.

'Seen the General?' he asked, as an acquaintance paused at his table to greet him.

'No, he hasn't been in today,' answered his friend. 'Good God, you don't want to see him, do you?'

Lowe smiled at the incredulity in the other's tone.

'Yes,' he said. 'I'd rather like a word with him.'

'A *word*!' exclaimed his fellow member feelingly. 'You'll be lucky if he lets you off with that.'

He passed on with a wave of his hand, and the dramatist poured himself out a second cup of tea and waited. It wasn't long before his patience was rewarded.

The swing door opened and the General marched in. There was no mistaking him. Anyone more like a stage representation of a General, Lowe had never seen. He was perfect in every detail: his close-cropped white hair, his lobster-coloured face, his fierce white moustache. Every detail was perfect, even to the monocle screwed in his left eye.

He came sailing towards his chair, nodding left and right, and sat down with a violent clearing of his throat. Lowe rose to his feet and threaded his way through the scattered chairs and tables to his side.

'Good afternoon, General,' he said pleasantly.

A fierce blue eye glared up at him.

'B'gad, Lowe!' said a hoarse voice thickly. 'How d'you do? Devilish long time since I've seen you!'

'It is some time. I've been very busy,' said the dramatist.

'Sit down. Sit down!' said Crayley-Watson, as though he was drilling a raw recruit. 'Writing anything new? B'gad! If you want plots I could tell you some stories of things I saw in India that 'ud make your hair stand on end!'

Lowe quite believed him. A great many of the members had suffered a similar sensation from the General's stories of India. He had no wish, however, to listen to Crayley Watson's interminable reminiscences, and before the old man could get started he interjected hastily:

'I've no doubt you could. By the way, I met a friend of yours yesterday. Lord Hillingdon.'

'Hillingdon? Hillingdon?' The General's eyebrows twitched. 'B'gad, yes! Nice chap. Knew his father very well. How is he?'

'Quite well,' said the dramatist, without in the least knowing whether Lord Hillingdon was well or otherwise.

'Nice feller!' said the General. 'I knew him when he was a boy. He must be getting on now. Bit wild as a youngster, gave his father no end of trouble. Got mixed up with a girl, and married her, b'gad! Old Hillingdon was furious.'

'Oh, yes,' murmured Lowe. 'I've heard something about that. An actress, wasn't she?'

'That's what she called herself,' retorted

Crayley-Watson. 'I shouldn't have done, though. Met some devilish fine actresses in my time. I remember when I was a youngster — '

'I was told she was an actress,' said Lowe, hastily warding off the threatened anecdote.

'Well, you were told wrong, sir,' said the General emphatically. 'She was a music-hall entertainer. A very different thing. Why young Chase married her is more than I can understand. I suppose he was infatuated. Darned young fool!'

'She died, didn't she?' said the dramatist, and the General nodded.

'Yes, just before the war,' he answered. 'Good thing for Chase. Well shot of her.'

'Did you ever meet her?' asked Lowe.

'No!' Crayley-Watson shook his head. 'Believe old Hillingdon met her. Luckily there were no children, would have been a catastrophe.'

'What did she die from?' queried Lowe, steering the conversation into the channel he wanted.

'Had a heart attack or something, I'm not quite sure,' said Crayley-Watson.

'Anyway, she died, and young Chase married a devilish fine girl. Eldest daughter of the Earl of Whitsey, a beauty if ever there was one.'

'What was his first wife, a dancer?' inquired the dramatist

'No, a blasted acrobat or something,' said the General disparagingly. 'She used to do a double turn with her brother. Forget what they called themselves. Young Chase met her while he was up at Oxford. She was giving a performance at a music hall there. And the next his father heard was that he'd married her. Blasted fool!'

There was nothing in all this that seemed remotely connected with the murders of Flood and Baldock, but Lowe was patient and persisted in the hope that he would be rewarded.

'What sort of a man is Hillingdon?' he asked casually.

'A fine feller. One of the old school! A real Pukka Sahib!' said the General. 'A fine soldier, too, B'gad! He was in my brigade during the war.' His frosty blue eyes suddenly widened and the monocle fell to the end of its silken cord. 'B'gad!

Of course, he lives at West Dorling, where those two fellers were killed. Read about it in *The Times*. Mentioned you, too, now I come to think of it.'

The dramatist bit his lip. He had hoped that Crayley-Watson would have been unaware of this.

'Devilish queer business,' continued the General, staring at him curiously. 'B'gad! You don't mean to tell me that Hillingdon is mixed up in it?' He leaned forward, breathing heavily in his excitement.

'No, no — ' began Lowe, but the General interrupted him.

'You can't fool me, Lowe,' he wheezed with a cunning wink. 'Wondered what you were getting at with all these questions about Hillingdon. B'gad!' He screwed the monocle back into his right eye. 'I remember now, the fellers were killed with arrows. Hillingdon used to be a fine archer — once saw him score nine golds in succession, in a competition, with my own eyes! Why did he kill those two fellers?'

'Really! I never said — ' Again Lowe

274

tried to stem the flow, but the old man was now well into his stride.

'A nod's as good as a wink to a blind man,' he said. 'When are you going to arrest him?'

'There's no question of an arrest,' said Lowe a little crossly. 'Really, General, I must ask you not to jump to — '

'That's all right! That's all right!' said the General. 'You needn't worry about my discretion, but I'm naturally interested.'

He almost licked his lips in anticipation of the tit-bit, which he would be able to relate to anyone with sufficient patience to listen to him.

'Good Gad! I wonder what made him do it?'

Lowe gave it up. He saw it was useless to argue. Brigadier General Crayley-Watson had got the idea firmly fixed in his head that Lord Hillingdon was a murderer, and nothing was likely to shift it.

'He must have had a good motive,' muttered the General. 'B'gad! I wonder — '
He stopped abruptly. 'Arrows! Arrows!' he said suddenly. 'These fellers were killed

with arrows. B'gad! I remember now! I remember, Lowe! Just come back to me! Those people, the music hall people. I remember what they called themselves. 'The Marvellous Arrows', that's it!'

Lowe sat up with a jerk.

'Are you sure of that?' he asked quickly.

'Sure? Of course I'm sure!' replied the General. 'Never make a statement unless I'm sure. Remember seeing a bill. 'The Marvellous Arrows', that's it! Can't think why I didn't remember it before.'

The dramatist was staring at him. Had he at last found a clue to the solution of the mystery?

24

The Variety Agent

There was nothing more to be learned from Crayley-Watson, and Lowe set about tactfully extricating himself from the clutches of the old man. This important item of information that had come to him so unexpectedly must be followed up immediately. But approaching the General and leaving him were two different things.

Eventually, however, the dramatist succeeded, and leaving the club he drove to Charing Cross Road, where he was presently received into the office of Mr. Isadore Gottlieb, a stout and pleasant faced man who greeted him with an expansive smile.

'Hello, Mr. Lowe!' he said. ''What's brought you here?'

'I wanted a little talk with you,' said the dramatist. 'How are you, Gottlieb?'

'I'm all right, but business is not too good.' The variety agent shook his head. 'The music hall business is dying out! Can't get the acts. Want to talk with me, do you? You're lucky to catch me, I was just going. Got to run down to Stratford to see a turn.'

'Well, I won't keep you very long,' said Lowe. 'It's quite a simple matter that I've come to see you about. Did you ever hear of an act calling themselves 'The Marvellous Arrows'?'

Gottlieb pursed his thick lips and frowned.

' 'The Marvellous Arrows'?' he repeated. 'Now let me see, Mr. Lowe. That must have been in the days before the war.'

'Yes, it was,' agreed the dramatist.

'I remember 'em,' said the agent, his face clearing. 'Got a memory like a filing cabinet, always had. Fellow and a girl, quite young they were. Used to do a variation of the old knife-throwing act. It was a novelty and they did very well.'

'What do you mean, a variation of the knife-throwing act?' asked Lowe.

'Instead of knives they used arrows,'

said Gottlieb. 'Glass arrows, and very effective they looked in the limes, too, I remember. The man used to stick the girl against a straw target and outline her with the things; shoot apples from her head, a la William Tell; shoot a cigarette from between her lips. All that kind of thing.' Lowe's eyes were gleaming and he felt his pulses quicken.

'What happened to them?' he asked.

'Dunno. They faded out,' said the variety agent. 'Believe the girl married an Earl or something. Good-looking couple they were.'

'Was Arrow their name?' asked Lowe.

Gottlieb shook his head.

'No, just a name they used for the act,' he answered. 'Can't remember what their name was.'

'You haven't a photograph I suppose?' said the dramatist, and again the variety agent shook his head.

'No, I haven't,' he replied. 'It's a long time ago now, Mr. Lowe. Nearly twenty-six years. I did have, but we turned out a lot of old stuff two or three years ago and all the old photographs were burned.'

'Could you tell me where I could get hold of one? It's rather important.'

Mr. Gottlieb wrinkled his forehead.

'I can tell you who might have one,' he said. 'Li Salmons.'

'Where can I find him?'

'Next block, third floor,' said Gottlieb laconically. 'I'll give you a note.' He scribbled rapidly on a sheet of paper, which he took from a rack in front of him, folded it, and slipped it into an envelope. 'Here you are, Mr, Lowe,' he said. 'What's the idea of these inquiries?'

'I'm looking into this business at West Dorling,' said the dramatist, and Mr. Gottlieb screwed up his face and whistled.

'By Jove, of course! I've read about that,' he said. 'Those two fellows who were killed with glass arrows. Good God! D'you think — '

'I don't think anything at the moment,' broke in Lowe hastily. 'I'm just following up a line of inquiry.'

Gottlieb nodded and his shrewd eyes twinkled.

'I get you,' he said. 'Well, try Salmons.

He may be able to help. I must dash off now.' He held out a podgy hand.

Mr. Salmons' offices in the next block were almost exactly similar to Gottlieb's. A girl in the outer office took the note and disappeared into an inner room. After a few seconds she returned.

'This way, please,' she said, and Lowe was ushered into the presence of Li Salmons.

He was a short man, with a florid complexion and large, dog-like brown eyes.

'Sit down, Mr. Lowe,' he said. 'Isadore Gottlieb suggests I may be able to help you. What is it?'

The dramatist explained, but to his disappointment Salmons shook his head.

'I've heard of the act, of course,' he said. 'But I haven't got a photograph. I don't know where you'll get one, unless — ' He nodded quickly. 'I'll tell you where you might,' he said. 'The stage door keeper who used to be at the old Oxford. He had one of the finest collections in London. Hobby of his.'

'Where can I find him?' said Lowe.

'He's working at the Magnifico, in Regent Street,' said Salmons. 'It's a picture theatre.'

'Thanks. I'll go along there,' said the dramatist. 'I'm very much obliged for your trouble.'

Mr. Salmons waved his hand.

'Only too glad to help any friend of old Gottlieb's,' he said. 'Collier is the name, by the way.'

Lowe went back to his car and drove to Regent Street.

The Magnifico was one of those ornate and ugly buildings which were springing up like mushrooms throughout the country. They ran a film programme, interspersed with a number of stage turns. An inquiry to the magnificently uniformed commissionaire in front sent Lowe round to the back where, in a narrow little box-like apartment, he discovered Collier.

Once again the dramatist explained his mission.

'I remember 'em,' said the old man. 'Brother and sister they was. Played at the old Oxford ever so many times.' He sighed. 'That was in the good old days,' he said sadly, 'when the music 'alls was music 'alls. Yes, I got a photograph, Mister, but it's round at my digs.'

'When will you be off duty?' inquired Lowe.

'Not afore ten,' said Mr. Collier, shaking his head. 'If you likes ter meet me 'ere just after ten, Mister, I'll take you round and show you the picture.'

'Where do you live?' asked the dramatist.

'T'other side of Westminster Bridge,' answered the stage door keeper. 'In the Kennington Road.'

'I'll be here at ten and wait for you,' said Lowe. He slipped a pound note into the maid's hand, and returning to his car drove slowly to Portland Place.

Arnold White received him with surprise.

'Hello!' he remarked. 'Holiday come to an end?' There was a twinkle of amusement in his eyes as he spoke.

'It came to an end,' said Lowe, 'before it started. Come on now, don't pretend you don't know why. You can read.'

'I nearly came down,' confessed the secretary. 'The papers have been splashing the business for days. Curious affair, isn't it? What do you make of it?'

'Up till today — nothing,' said his employer. 'But more or less by accident I think I've hit on something that's going to solve the problem.'

He gave an account of his interview with Crayley-Watson and all it had led to. White listened with interest, his eyes wide.

'You seem to have stumbled on the hub of the whole affair,' he commented, when the dramatist had finished. 'I shouldn't think there's any doubt that the brother of the girl is the man you want.'

'I don't think there's any doubt, either,' agreed Lowe. 'That seems clear enough. The question is, what is his motive?'

'If you get the man you'll get the motive, too,' said White, not without reason. 'I should think, personally, that these men, Flood, Baldock arid Dinsley have done something to injure this fellow, and it's a case of revenge.'

'That's my impression, too,' said his

employer. 'Hence the use of the glass arrows. At the same time we can't eliminate the possibility of Hillingdon being guilty. He married the woman and there's a possibility that he may be the killer for the same reason. However,' — he took out his pipe and began to stuff tobacco into the charred bowl — 'it's useless speculating until I've seen this photograph.'

There were a number of things which White had to discuss with him, and this occupied, with dinner, a greater part of the time that he had to fill in before he was due to pick up Collier. When he reached the Magnifico he found the old man waiting at the stage door.

'Got a car, have you,' he remarked, as Lowe led him over to the big machine. 'It's a long time since I've ridden in one of them things. I'll sit beside you, Mister. It'll be easier to direct you.'

In twenty minutes they had crossed Westminster Bridge and were running along the beginning of Kennington Road.

'Here we are,' said the old man suddenly, pointing to an old-fashioned house on the right.

Lowe brought the car into the kerb and halted opposite.

'Come in, Mister,' said Collier, getting down, and Lowe followed him across the strip of pavement, up the narrow path to the front door.

The old man let himself in with a key, and ushered his visitor up a flight of stairs to a landing. Opening a door on the left he stood aside for the dramatist to enter, and pressed down a light switch.

Lowe found himself in a large room, furnished as a bed sitting room, and decorated in a surprising manner. The entire walls were literally covered with photographs. There must have been hundreds, and each one was signed with the name of a music hall star or stage celebrity.

Old Collier surveyed his collection proudly.

'There's the work o' years there, Mister,' he said. 'They always used to give me a photograph. Them was the days, and they won't come again. You can't get signed pictures off a blinkin' screen.' He went over to a portion of a wall beside the bed and pointed. 'That's the picture you want, Mister,' he said, and Lowe bent forward.

It was a large, glossy photograph representing a slim, pretty girl in spangled tights, and a young man in the costume of Robin Hood, holding in his hand a large bow.

Lowe drew in his breath sharply as he saw the face and his expression changed to one of amazement and incredulity.

'That's what you want, Mister, ain't it?'

'That's what I want!' breathed the dramatist.

He had found the Glass Arrow murderer!

25

The Last Killing

Mr. John Dinsley sat in his study and examined the possibilities of his future critically and with care. During the last twenty-four hours he had been a very busy man indeed. The arrangements for his flight were complete down to the last detail. There only remained now to collect the money from Hillingdon and go.

He had said nothing to his daughter about his intentions. She must fend for herself. He was aware of the intimacy that existed between her and Alan Wargreave and was not the least worried about her future. She would be well looked after.

He was sorry now that he had given Hillingdon so much time. Every day meant a greater risk, and the police were busy and vigilant. At any moment they might discover something and then

— goodbye to all chance of escape.

He looked an old man as he sat nibbling at his fingers and going over and over again in his mind the plans he had made. At present they were all in embryo. He had put none of them into practice, for the slightest inkling of what he intended to do would bring his schemes toppling about his head. There would be time enough when he had left West Dorling for good. A man with money generally gets what he wants, and he reckoned on at least a twenty-four hour start. It should be sufficient. By that time he would be out of the country.

The light outside had gone from the sky, but he made no attempt to light the room. The darkness suited him.

Suddenly into the silence came the jarring note of the telephone bell, and he started and frowned. Who could be ringing up? It was after nine. The bell continued to shrill its warning, and hesitantly he stretched out his hand and picked up the receiver.

'Hello!' A faint whispering voice reached him. 'Hello! Is that John Dinsley?'

'Who are you?' demanded Dinsley curtly.

'This is Hillingdon,' said the voice rapidly.

'Oh! I can scarcely hear you,' said Dinsley. 'Speak louder.'

'I can't,' was the reply. 'I'm afraid somebody might hear. Listen. I have the money. I arranged with my bank this morning and I've got in cash all you asked. Meet me at the same place at half past ten and I'll give it to you.'

'Right!' said Dinsley. 'Half past ten in Elmer Lane.'

He put the instrument back on its rack and expelled his breath slowly. This was an unexpected piece of good fortune. He had never anticipated that Hillingdon would have the money before the date he had arranged. This meant there would be no delay. He could put forward his plans at once.

Rapidly he revised his original intentions. He would go at half past ten and collect the money, come back, pack the few articles he intended taking with him, and by midnight shake the dust of West Dorling from his feet for good. He would make for Heston, charter a 'plane, and before dawn broke he ought to be across the channel.

He rose, lit a cigarette, and began to pace up and down the room nervously. It couldn't have happened better . . .

The watcher outside yawned wearily. Another long session of fruitless vigil, thought Detective Constable Higson, as he stood in the shadow of the shrubbery from whence he could cover all approaches to the house. Hours to go yet before his relief would arrive. The fellow who said a policeman's life was not a happy one certainly knew something, and this stupid business of watching a man who never went anywhere or did anything worth watching seemed likely to go on interminably. He was thoroughly fed up and the bushes rustled behind him and he swung round, startled, but he could see nothing. A rabbit, probably, he thought disgustedly. There were plenty of them.

He turned back facing the house, and the figure that crept up softly behind him made no sound on the springy turf. A hand holding a pad of reeking cotton

wool was clapped over Higson's mouth
and nostrils and an arm under his chin
jerked back his head.

He made a desperate effort to struggle
free, but the attack had been sudden and
he was unprepared. His efforts only drew
the drug quicker into his lungs, and in a
few seconds he was hanging limp and
senseless in the arms of the man who had
come out of the blackness of the night . . .

John Dinsley left the house as a clock
was striking ten. He left by the windows
of his study, and passing swiftly down the
drive emerged into the narrow road.
There was no one about and the night
was still and starlit. Walking rapidly, he
reached Elmer Lane, turned into the
twisting track, and made his way towards
the stile where he had previously held his
brief conversation with Hillingdon.

The silence was intense, a silence that
only the country can supply. He rested his
elbows on the wooden bar of the barrier
and waited.

Five minutes passed . . . ten . . . he
frowned. Hillingdon was late. He heard
no sound of approaching footsteps, but

suddenly, without warning, a figure stood before him.

'So you've come at last!' he grunted ungraciously.

'I have come at last!' whispered a voice. 'I came to Flood and I came to Baldock. And now, John Dinsley, I have come to you!'

Dinsley gave a gulp and his throat went dry with terror.

'What — what do you mean?' His voice was a cracked and husky whisper. 'Who are you?'

'I am the son of the man who died in a shell-hole in Flanders,' said the voice and Dinsley staggered back, his face grey.

'Lane!' The name came in a whisper of horror and fear, a barely audible whisper that floated like a sighing breath on the stillness.

'Yes, Lane!' said the voice sternly, and Dinsley looked wildly around. Where was Hillingdon? If only he would arrive . . .

At that moment the terrified man would willingly have forfeited the fifty-thousand pounds for a sight of the man whose life he had ruined.

The dim figure before him seemed to read his thoughts.

'If you're looking for Hillingdon,' it said, 'you will be disappointed. He will not come, either now or ever! Earlier this evening I saw him and I left him a happier and wiser man.'

'He — he phoned me,' began Dinsley tremulously.

'*I* phoned you,' broke in the other. 'You have come to the end, Dinsley.'

Dinsley licked his dry lips. His fear made speech difficult, but he managed with an effort to gain control over the numbed muscles of his throat.

'Lane — Lane died in the war,' he mumbled. 'He was killed by a German bullet. You can't blame me for that.'

'He was killed with an English bullet!' said the other. 'He was murdered, Dinsley, by you and Flood and Baldock. Robbed and left to be buried in a nameless grave.'

'You're wrong! You're wrong!' panted Dinsley. 'Who told you this?'

'That doesn't matter!' snapped the voice. 'I know!'

'I had no hand in it!' The grey-haired man was cringing — an obscene, mouthing thing in his terror. 'I had no hand in it! It was Baldock and Flood! It was *their* idea, not mine. I didn't want them to do it!'

'You were all in it together. You all three benefited, and therefore you are all equally guilty!' retorted the unknown.

'I swear to you' — the hoarse voice was high-pitched and quavering — 'I swear to you that I had no hand in it!'

'And Ollen? You had no hand in that, either, I suppose?' said the other remorselessly. 'You ran Ollen down in your car, and when you found that had failed, that there was a chance of his recovering consciousness, you came in the night to the room where he lay and stabbed him!'

'I — I — how do you know all this?' Dinsley was breathless.

'Never mind. I do know. You killed Gormley, too. You have three murders on your soul, John Dinsley, and you're going to pay the penalty for one of them tonight!'

'No! No! Lane, listen!' whimpered Dinsley, half-crazy with fright. 'You can't do that! You mustn't do that! I'll do anything — '

'Nothing you can do,' said the man called Lane, 'will make any difference. I have waited for twenty years for this moment, and it has come at last!'

Dinsley gave a hoarse cry, inarticulate and animal-like, and launched himself at the figure before him. But the man sidestepped, and he went blundering past, carried forward by the force of his spring. As he checked his forward rush, recovered his balance and turned, he heard a twang like the plucking of a double bass string. A sharp, agonizing pain shot through his left side, and the darkness of the night blended with the greater darkness of death . . .

26

The Sparrow

Trevor Lowe came back to West Dorling early in the afternoon of the following day, to find the village in an uproar over the latest murder.

Dinsley's body had been discovered by a labourer on his way to work, and Detective-Inspector Shadgold, Noyes and the Chief Constable were in conference when the dramatist was shown into the Inspector's little office at Middlethorpe police station.

'Glad you've got back, Mr. Lowe,' greeted Shadgold fervently. 'Have you heard the latest?'

'Mrs. Jiffer told me when I called at the cottage,' said the dramatist.

Major Harland pursed his lips.

'Something must be done to stop this unknown killer,' he said. 'Nobody's safe while he's at large. We don't know who'll be the next.'

'There'll be no next,' said Lowe calmly. 'Dinsley was the last.'

'How can you be sure of that?' demanded Shadgold irritably.

'Because I know the murderer,' answered the dramatist simply.

There was general consternation. The Chief Constable's mouth dropped open in a ludicrous expression of surprise. Inspector Noyes emitted an appalling series of hisses and grunts, while Shadgold stared, petrified with astonishment.

'You — you know the murderer?' he gasped weakly. 'Is this a joke, Mr. Lowe?'

'Certainly not,' said the dramatist gravely. 'The man responsible for these killings is called Lane. He and his sister were, in the days before the war, a music hall act calling themselves 'The Marvellous Arrows'. They used to put up a show similar to the well-known knife-throwing act, only instead of knives the man used glass arrows.'

'How did you discover this, Mr. Lowe?' Inspector Noyes had recovered his voice and bellowed the question so loudly that the Chief Constable started.

Lowe told them.

'And this woman was Hillingdon's first wife?' said Major Harland.

The dramatist nodded.

'Who's this man Lane?' grunted Shadgold. 'The sooner we pull him in the better.'

'He won't be difficult to find,' said Lowe coolly.

'I suppose you're going to say you know where he is?' growled the Scotland Yard man, and to their surprise the dramatist nodded.

'I do,' he answered.

'Then we'll arrest him at once,' declared Shadgold, rising to his feet. 'Where is he, Mr. Lowe?'

'Just a minute.' Lowe held up his hand. 'There's plenty of time to arrest Lane, and there are several details I want to clear up first.'

'But in the meantime, Mr. Lowe,' protested the Chief Constable, 'the man may clear off.'

'You needn't worry about that, Major,' said Lowe confidently. 'He hasn't the least idea that we suspect him.'

'Where is he?' asked Noyes. 'In the district?'

'Oh, yes, he's in the district,' said the dramatist. 'You know him quite well.'

'We — we know him?' stuttered the Chief Constable, his face scarlet with excitement. 'I must insist, sir, that you tell us the name of this man at once!'

'I've already done so,' said Lowe. 'His name is Lane.'

'Yes. Yes!' said Major Harland impatiently. 'That is his real name. But what is the name under which we know him?'

'I'm not going to tell you that — yet,' said Lowe. 'As I said, there are several details which, for my own satisfaction, I wish to clear up, and a precipitate move would probably destroy all chance of my doing so.'

'But don't you realize — ' The military side of the Chief Constable was getting the upper hand. 'Don't you realize, sir, that you may be jeopardizing the course of justice?'

'I realize nothing except that I'm handling this affair, and I'll handle it my own way!' retorted Lowe.

300

'I think,' interposed Shadgold, as he saw that the Chief Constable was in imminent danger of an attack of apoplexy, 'that we can safely leave this to Mr. Lowe. I have worked with him on many occasions and I can confidently state that he wouldn't do anything that was likely to result in our losing our man.'

Lowe shot him a grateful glance.

'Thanks for the testimonial, Shadgold,' he said. 'And I assure you that you're right. There's no danger of any more killings, or of this man trying to make a premature getaway. If you'll leave the whole thing to me I promise you that at the right moment I will reveal the name of the murderer of Dinsley, Flood and Baldock.'

'What about these other three men?' demanded the Chief Constable.

'Ollen, Gormley, and Viness,' interjected Inspector Noyes.

'I don't think Lane was responsible for the killing of Ollen or Gormley,' answered Lowe. 'Viness I'm not sure about. That's one of the things I want to clear up. I don't know how he comes into it at all.'

'Well, sir,' said the Chief Constable, frowning heavily, 'I must say that I strongly disapprove. If Inspector Shadgold is willing to take the responsibility I am prepared to allow you twenty-four hours. At the end of that time I must insist that you tell us who this man is.'

'I'll take the responsibility, sir,' said Shadgold quietly, and that was practically the end of the matter.

Later, when they left Middlethorpe police station to return to Medlock's cottage, the Inspector looked at his friend.

'If anything does happen and this fellow gets away, Mr. Lowe,' he said, 'you're going to get me into serious trouble. You know that?'

'And you know,' said Lowe, 'that if there was any danger of that I wouldn't withhold the information. I'll admit I'm doing so from a purely selfish view. I want the whole story, and I don't think, if this man Lane was arrested in the ordinary way, I should get it. Where's Medlock?'

'He's dashing about the village getting information for his confounded paper,' snorted Shadgold. 'He says this is the

302

most marvellous story that any reporter ever had to deal with. Talks about it as if it was a piece of statuary or a picture or something.'

The dramatist smiled.

'He's got the reporter's instinct,' he said. 'It appeals to his sense of the dramatic. How was it Dinsley managed to elude the man who was watching him?'

'The man who was watching him,' grunted the Inspector, 'was chloroformed and trussed up and left helpless in the shrubbery. We didn't find him until two hours after the discovery of the body.'

'You searched Dinsley's house, of course?' said the dramatist.

Shadgold nodded.

'Yes, but there was nothing,' he answered.

'And the girl — the daughter — what's happened to her?' went on Lowe.

'She's still at the house,' replied Shadgold. 'It gave her a shock, but she's not very upset. Immediately the news became known a young fellow by the name of Wargreave called. He's Lord Hillingdon's secretary, and he managed to cheer her up a bit. I think they're engaged or something. Look here, why not tell me the whole strength of this? I give you my word I won't take any action until you say. Is it a bet?'

The dramatist considered for a moment.

'Yes, it's a bet,' he answered. 'Now listen.'

Almost at his first words Shadgold stopped dead and eyed him incredulously.

'Good God!' he said. 'You don't mean it?'

'I do!' replied the dramatist gravely. 'And there's no doubt. I've got his photograph in my pocket!'

★ ★ ★

'There!' said Tom Medlock, with a sigh of relief, pulling a sheet of paper out of his typewriter. 'That's that.'

'Finished, Tom?' asked Trevor Lowe, looking up from the book he was reading.

'Yes, thank the Lord,' said the reporter, rising to his feet and stretching himself. 'How d'you like my headlines?' He tossed the manuscript over to his friend and

Lowe glanced at the top page. Across it in capitals ran:

WHO IS THE SPARROW?
UNKNOWN ARROW MURDERER
CAUSES PANIC IN VILLAGE
THIRD VICTIM WELL-KNOWN
RESIDENT

With the discovery of the body of Mr. John Dinsley, of Highfield House, West Dorling, the Sparrow has added a third victim to his —

'Still running on the old fairy tale, I see,' said the dramatist, looking up.

'I've been running on it all the time,' answered Medlock, helping himself to a cigarette. 'It was sticking out a mile. The method of the murders shouted for it. 'Who killed cock robin? I, said the sparrow, with my bow and arrow.' You couldn't have had anything more fitting.'

He winced suddenly and pressed a hand to his side. Lowe saw his face go white and his forehead shone damply in the light.

'Nasty twinge that,' muttered Medlock

breathlessly. 'I've had several of them lately.'

'It's all this excitement,' said the dramatist. 'The doctors told you not to excite yourself, Tom.'

'Oh, well, I've enjoyed it.' Medlock sat down a little abruptly and his eyes were clouded with pain. 'This is the last reporting job I shall ever do, so I might as well do it well. Did you do any good in Town?'

Lowe nodded.

'Yes. I got hold of some very useful information,' he answered.

'I've been meaning to ask you,' said the reporter, 'but I haven't had a chance all day. Is it anything you can give me?'

'Not for publication,' answered the dramatist. 'At least, not yet.'

'That sounds as though you've struck something,' said Medlock interestedly.

'Yes, I think I have,' admitted his friend. 'I think I've found your sparrow.'

'You have!' The reporter sat up with a jerk. 'You mean that, Lowe?'

'Yes. I mean it.' The dramatist laid aside his book, rose to his feet, and

306

walked over to the mantelpiece. 'I've found the sparrow, Tom, but I don't know the why and the wherefore.'

'Well, that shouldn't be difficult to discover once you've got the man,' said Medlock.

'No, I agree with you,' replied Lowe. 'Tell me, Tom. Why did you kill those three men?'

27

An Echo From Flanders

Tom Medlock removed the cigarette from between his lips and blew out a little stream of smoke.

'How did you find out, Lowe?' he inquired quietly.

For answer the dramatist put his hand into his breast pocket and produced an envelope. From it he took the photograph that had graced Mr. Collier's collection.

'I see.' The reporter nodded. 'I was wondering if you would find out, you know. I speculated over it quite a lot, but I thought I'd been careful enough to obliterate every clue.'

'You were — with the exception of this,' said Lowe, 'and I only discovered this by accident.'

Medlock flung the end of his cigarette into the grate, took another from his case, and lit it.

'I suppose you want to hear the whole story?' he remarked conversationally.

'I'd like to know the 'Why',' said Lowe.

Medlock examined the end of his cigarette critically, his brows drawn over his eyes.

'It goes back a few years,' he said, after a moment's silence. 'To just before the war, as a matter of fact. I killed those men, Lowe, because they murdered my father.' He drew in a mouthful of smoke, inhaled deeply, and went on before Lowe could speak: 'My real name is Lane — you know that — my father was an illusionist — a conjurer. I daresay you've heard of him, the Great Devine.'

The dramatist nodded.

'My mother died in giving birth to Joyce, my sister,' continued the reporter, 'and father had to look after us entirely on his own. He took us round with him on his various tours, and we were brought up in an atmosphere of lights and greasepaint. So it wasn't surprising that when we were old enough we should enter the same profession as our parents — mother was a soubrette when father married her. He had a number of glass arrows which he bought in an antique shop in Venice — I think he had a vague idea at the time of working them into one of his illusions — however, nothing came of it, but it gave me the idea for an original act.

'Joyce and I practised and practised — we didn't use the glass arrows until we were proficient — and eventually father's influence got us a trial date and we were an immediate success.

'The agent who booked our act, a man called Montague Linden, fell for Joyce, and they were married at Christmas of nineteen hundred and eleven. It wasn't a happy marriage, and twelve months later Joyce left him. He got into difficulties soon after and disappeared, and we heard he'd been killed in a railway accident.'

He paused long enough to light a cigarette from the stump of the old one and then went on:

'In the early part of nineteen thirteen Joyce met Lord Hillingdon. He was Hilary Chase then. They were married six months later. There was some trouble from the old Earl, but Chase behaved very decently. His father, after his first not unnatural outburst, rather grudgingly accepted the situation, and after some time Joyce settled down to her new life quite happily. We heard from her now and again and her letters were always full of her husband's kindness. Then the war broke out.'

Medlock stopped abruptly.

'You might give me a drink, old man. All this talking is dry work.'

Lowe went over to the side table and poured out some whisky.

'Thanks.' The reporter swallowed half the contents and rested the glass on his knee. 'That's better. Where was I? Oh, yes. The war.

'Joyce had been ill — she was always delicate, the same trouble as I've got, I think — and Chase sent her over to the South of France for her health. She was there when war was declared, and he was ordered to join his regiment. She never came back to England, and he never saw her again. I expect you're wondering what all this has to do with Dinsley, Flood and Baldock, but I'm coming to that soon.

'It was six months later when we heard that Joyce was dead. By the time the news reached us she had already been buried. It was Chase who informed us, and he was terribly cut up. She had died suddenly in the street, and there was nothing to identify her. It was only when she was discovered to be missing from her hotel for some days that they realized who she was, and by then she had been buried as an unknown.

'I don't think, except for the feverish excitement of those days of the war, such a thing could have happened. But it did.

'Chase went to the front soon after, came back on leave, and married his present wife, under the firm belief that he was a widower.

'In the meanwhile my father had joined up — I tried to, but was rejected on medical grounds — and was almost immediately drafted to the front. For some years he had made a hobby of collecting diamonds. He had invested all his savings, and they were considerable, in this way, and kept the stones in a safe, which he rented in the Fetter Lane deposit. 'They're always convertible into cash, and I don't trust banks, anyway' was his argument.

'He had bought a lot of stones from two men who had been introduced to him by Montague Linden. They called themselves John Burton and Geoffrey Hillock then, but they'll be more familiar to you under the names they took later.'

'Dinsley and Baldock,' murmured Lowe. Medlock nodded.

'Yes. We're coming to it, you see,' he said. 'You'll see everything clearly in a minute or so.'

'Altogether I suppose my father had accumulated about seven or eight thousand pounds' worth of diamonds, and the key to the safe and the code word which was necessary to gain admittance to the depository he carried in a little case next to his skin, and this was to lead to his death. But I'll come to that in its proper order.

'I had always been keen on writing, and began to consider taking it up seriously. I wrote one or two stories under the name of Tom Medlock and sold them, which encouraged me to do more. I was in the middle of one when there came a ring at the door of my little flat, which I'd taken in Bloomsbury, and when I went to see who it was I recognized Joyce!

'You can imagine my surprise. She was in a pitiful state, in rags, and scarcely recognizable. I took her in and gave her some food, and then she told me what had happened. She had been out for a walk when suddenly she had come face-to-face with Montague Linden. He had recognized her at once, and insisted on taking her to tea at a café. He had heard of her marriage to Chase.

' 'I suppose you know,' he said, 'that you're in a very unpleasant position. You've committed bigamy'.

'She protested that it had been unwittingly, but he terrified her so that she agreed to his proposal that she should come back to him there and then. They left the same night for Paris, and there they stayed, he constantly holding over her head the threat of exposure.

'One day he brought her a newspaper

314

and showed her the account of her husband's marriage to the Earl of Whitsey's daughter.

'That may be useful when the old man dies and he inherits the title', he said.

'He soon tired of the renewed association, and one day she found him gone. There's no need for me to go into an account of her sufferings or how she managed to earn a precarious living in a strange country. Eventually she fell ill, and believing that she hadn't much longer to live she came to England, and after a lot of difficulty found where I was living.

'I wanted to inform Chase, but she begged me not to. 'He's married and happy', she said. 'What good can it do?'

'I called in a doctor, and when he told me she had barely a month to live I couldn't see what good it would do, either. I acceded to her request. I took her to the country in the name of Medlock and there she died. She died on the day that the newspaper published the fact that a son had been born to Hilary Chase.

'The war dragged on. My father came home for several leaves, and I told him about Joyce, and he agreed with me that it was better to keep it to ourselves.

'Up till then — it was nineteen-seventeen — my father had gone through the war without a scratch. I had a letter from him after his last leave in which he said: 'Who d'you think we've got here? Those two fellows, John Burton and Geoffrey Hillock. They've been conscripted, and they don't appear to like it. Still, I doubt if the whole business can last much longer.'

'A month or two later he wrote again. 'Hillock and Burton have settled down, but they're scared to death every time a big one comes over.'

'That was the last time I ever heard from him. He was reported missing in the next offensive, and daily I waited anxiously for news. But none came.

'I consulted a solicitor regarding the safe deposit and the diamonds which I knew were there. He was dubious. My father had left no will, and anyway, we would have to get the court's permission to presume death before I could claim the contents of the safe. It was unlikely we should get it, since my father might turn up at any moment. It was possible that he had been taken prisoner of war.

'I continued with my writing, doing better and better, and became friendly with the news editor of the *Megaphone*. He suggested I should do a series of crime articles, and he was so pleased, with the result that he commissioned a further series right away.

'The Armistice came, and there was still no news of my father. Again I went to the solicitor, and he suggested we should go round and interview the manager of the safe deposit. We did, and here I got a shock, for the safe had been cleared. A man armed with the key and the code word had presented himself a month previously. From the description I had no difficulty in recognizing Hillock. I knew then that my father was dead.'

There was a little interval of silence as Medlock lit another cigarette.

'I could only guess at what had happened, but it was not until much later, during the last few days, as a matter of fact, that I discovered how much worse the truth was to what I had imagined. I believed then that my father had been killed in action and that these men had merely robbed his body. It was Preston Flood who told me the truth just before he died.'

'Preston Flood?' asked Lowe inquiringly.

'I've referred to him as Montague Linden,' said Medlock, and the dramatist understood.

'I tried to trace Hillock and Burton, for I guessed they were both in it, but without result.

'There's very little more to tell. You know how I became a crime reporter, and how my health broke down and I had to give it up and go back to writing articles and stories, how I eventually wrote a successful novel and bought this place. What you don't know and what nobody else knew was that I was always hoping to find Hillock and Burton and Linden.

'Well, at last I found them. They'd been here some time before I associated them with the men I was seeking,' he continued, 'and then it was Flood who gave himself away.

'Linden had had a mannerism. When he was thinking or worried he had a habit of running his thumbnail up and down the space between his lower middle teeth. It was a small thing, but it was enough. Although they had all three changed almost beyond recognition, once I had an inkling of who they were it wasn't difficult.

'I still had five of the arrows which we'd used in the act, and I decided that I'd use three of them for the purpose of killing these men who had robbed my father.'

'A sense of the dramatic, eh?' murmured Lowe, and Medlock smiled faintly.

'It was a month ago that I discovered who they really were,' he went on, 'and I'd made my plans when you nearly spoilt everything by wiring to say you were coming. I'd almost decided to put it off, and then I thought what an alibi your presence offered.'

'You put through the telephone call, I suppose,' said Lowe, 'that took Flood to the ruins?'

Medlock nodded.

'Yes,' he answered. 'I got up early, put the arrows and a bow in my golf bag, and drove to the call box. I left the car round the corner in the lane and walked the short distance from there to the box. I addressed Flood by the name of Linden, refused to give my own name, but said it was most important for his own sake that I should see him. He came, and I was waiting for him.

'I accused him, with his two associates, of robbing my father, and in his fear he told me the truth. He said he'd had no hand in it, that it was Baldock's idea. The three of them had been drafted to the same regiment, and during a barrage they had found themselves in a shell-hole with my father. He had several times discussed the diamonds with Dinsley and Baldock, he had no reason to suspect them of being anything else but straightforward dealers, and he mentioned that he carried the key and the code word on him.

'Baldock had shot him, stripped the body of all means of identification, and taken the key and the paper with the word that would admit the bearer to the safe deposit.

They had reckoned that amid that saturnalia of death the murder would go undetected, as it did.

'Flood told me this in an outburst of fear to try and save his own skin, for I think he saw by my expression what I intended to do. But it didn't save him, it only made me see red. I killed him with as little compunction as I would have trodden on a slug.

'I hurried back to the cottage. If you had been up I should have said that I'd been out on the links practising putting. But you weren't, and everything was plain sailing.

'I deliberately took you to the ruins so that together we could discover the body of Flood, and when you and Inspector Noyes went to Flood's house I occupied part of the time before I turned up in killing Baldock. I adopted the same method. I telephoned him and repeated what I'd said to Flood, except I suggested he should come to the wall gate.

'Why did you open Flood's safe?' asked Lowe.

Medlock shook his head.

'I didn't do that,' he answered. 'That was Gormley. Gormley, who was always poking and prying about, followed Flood to the ruins and saw me kill him. He tried to blackmail me, having safeguarded himself by writing a full account of what he had seen and depositing it with Viness.'

'And yet, knowing this, you took the risk of killing him?' said the dramatist.

Again the reporter shook his head.

'No, I didn't kill Gormley,' he answered. 'Dinsley did that because he knew of the hold they had on Hillingdon and that they were blackmailing him. I was in a panic when I heard of Gormley's death, but Viness' greed saved me. Instead of forwarding the statement to the police he tried a little blackmail on his own account.

'He came down and arranged to meet me, boasting of the statement in his safe. I saw that my only safeguard was to kill him, and I did, taking his keys so that I could secure the document and burn it.'

'So when you were supposed to be in London you were in West Dorling all the time?' murmured Lowe. 'How does Ollen come into all this?'

'Poor Ollen,' said Medlock. 'He was with Dinsley, Baldock and Flood at the front. He recognized Dinsley and tackled him with being the John Burton that he knew. Dinsley was scared that he might spread it about the village, and tried to run him down. When that failed and he learned that there was a chance of Ollen recovering consciousness he killed him.'

'And they were blackmailing Hillingdon,' said the dramatist, 'by holding this bigamy charge over his head?'

'Yes,' said Medlock. 'Last night I went to see him and set his mind at rest. He had been worried to death for fear his son was illegitimate. That's what they worked on.'

'Of course Flood, or Linden, supplied them with the information,' said Lowe. 'But why did they waste such a long time?'

'They weren't in England,' said the reporter. 'After the war, when they had collected the diamonds from the safe deposit, they went to Australia, and there they remained until the money was gone.'

'What surprises me,' said the dramatist,

frowning slightly, 'is why Dinsley didn't associate the glass arrow with you.'

'Neither he nor Baldock had very much to do with me,' explained Medlock. 'Flood would have known, but he was dead. I don't think the others had ever seen our act.'

'I see.'

There was a long silence, and then Medlock, who had been staring at the floor, looked up.

'What are you going to do, Lowe?' he said simply.

'I'm going to do nothing until the morning.' The dramatist spoke slowly. 'I'm more sorry than I can say, Tom.'

'Does anyone know but you?' murmured the reporter.

'Shadgold knows,' said Lowe. 'But he won't take any official action until the morning.'

He looked steadily at his friend, and an expression of understanding came into Medlock's eyes.

'We'll go to bed, shall we?' he said. 'It's getting late.'

Mrs. Jiffer found him, and he looked very peaceful. The little tube of morphine tablets on his bedside table was empty.

'You knew he was going to do this, Mr. Lowe,' accused Shadgold, when he heard, and the dramatist made no effort to deny it.

'I hoped he would, Shadgold,' he said. 'After all, he's paid the penalty. Death is the payment for death, whether it's by the rope or otherwise.'

'Well,' the Inspector shrugged his shoulders, 'the case is over anyway. Dinsley's daughter must have known. You remember telling me how scared she was when she heard about the arrows.'

Lowe nodded, his expression puzzled.

'Yes, that's the only thing I don't understand,' he said. 'She couldn't have known. She must have had some other reason.'

'Well, it doesn't matter,' said Shadgold. 'It isn't important, anyway.'

'You see, darling,' said Alan Wargreave that evening to Ilene Dinsley when the village was seething with news. 'You frightened yourself sick over nothing. Nobody's found out that I know anything about archery, after all.'

Tom Medlock had left a bulky letter addressed to Lowe, which contained several sheets of typing paper and a short note.

'Dear Lowe,' it ran. '*This will save a lot of trouble. I have written a full account practically as I told you. Will you see that it is sent to Bishop of 'The Wire'? Goodbye, and thanks for the opportunity,*
            T.M.'

The Wire came out with the full story the following day. Tom Medlock's last scoop was the biggest of his career.

THE END

We do hope that you have enjoyed reading this large print book.

Did you know that all of our titles are available for purchase?

We publish a wide range of high quality large print books including:
**Romances, Mysteries, Classics
General Fiction
Non Fiction and Westerns**

Special interest titles available in large print are:
**The Little Oxford Dictionary
Music Book, Song Book
Hymn Book, Service Book**

Also available from us courtesy of Oxford University Press:
**Young Readers' Dictionary
(large print edition)
Young Readers' Thesaurus
(large print edition)**

For further information or a free brochure, please contact us at:
**Ulverscroft Large Print Books Ltd.,
The Green, Bradgate Road, Anstey,
Leicester, LE7 7FU, England.
Tel:** (00 44) 0116 236 4325
Fax: (00 44) 0116 234 0205

Other titles in the
Linford Mystery Library:

THE TWISTED TONGUES

John Burke

A wartime traitor who broadcast from Germany is finally released from prison. Nobody wanted to listen to him during the war and nobody wants to listen to him now. But he intends to be heard, and when he begins to write his memoirs for a newspaper, old ghosts stir uneasily and it becomes a race against time: will he reveal the truth behind the smug respectability of men in high places before they find a means of silencing him forever?

ANGEL DOLL

Arlette Lees

It's the dark days of the Great Depression, and former Boston P.D. detective Jack Dunning is starting over after losing both his wife and his job to the bottle. Fresh off the Greyhound, he slips into The Blue Rose Dance Hall — and falls hard for a beautiful dime-a-dance girl, Angel Doll. But then Angel shoots gangster Axel Teague and blows town on the midnight train to Los Angeles . . .

THE INFERNAL DEVICE

Michael Kurland

Professor Moriarty, erstwhile Mathematics professor, is not 'the greatest rogue unhanged' that Sherlock Holmes would have one believe, but rather an amoral genius — and the only man Holmes has ever been bested by. *The Infernal Device* takes Professor Moriarty from London to Stamboul to Moscow and back, Sherlock Holmes close on his tail, until they both join forces to pursue and capture a man more devious and more dangerous than either of them has ever faced before . . .